A
SONG
OF
SOUL

T.R. DURANT

Editors: Vicki Knedgen and Elizabeth Gardner
Cover Design: Getcovers
Formatting: RedFox Book Design

** WARNING **
This book contains sexually explicit scenes, violence, kink and adult language that may be offensive to some readers. It is intended for adults 18 and over.

FOREWORD

This book is written in British English, so a few words might be spelled differently from what some readers are used to.

Don't let the sweet blurb trick you, this is a smutty book. In fact, this is smut on a stick. It has a plot, but the main thing is SMUT. My books are normally like a layered cake—with layers of world-building, plot, character development, steamy scenes, etc. This is a lollipop, the smut is the candy and the plot is the stick. Now that you've been warned, it is time to decide if you want to grab an extra pair of panties and suck this spicy candy or not.

If you stick with us, I hope you enjoy Samantha and Collins's sweet smutty story. They definitely enjoyed each other.

HOME

Samantha

Home. I've never belonged
There was never a person or place
I could call home
But somewhere in my dreams
In the songs playing within,
I knew I had a place to be

Maybe a life dreamt or forgotten
As if left underwater
Only its echoes reaching me
But the hums and the rhythm
Even quieted by oblivion
Screamed louder than reality
So here have I always been
Lost in a song and a dream
Trying to reconcile this routine
With the sea I've never seen

CHAPTER 1

Samantha

The water splashes out of the swimming pool as I jump in. Sitting at the bottom, I hug my legs and watch dainty bubbles leave my mouth. Silence embraces me, and I let the echoes of the upbeat tunes from dance class fade away. I love the reticence of being underwater just as much as I love music. For me, there is always a song in silence.

I hold my breath until everything disappears from my mind but the pleasant humming that has been following my dreams since I can remember. An unknown song that feels far more familiar than anything I know—the swimming pool, the rec centre, or any grasp of reality surrounding me.

I let the song lull me, possess me with its striking crescendos, and soothe my mind with its melancholic finale. While I sing in my mind, it's so peaceful here without any white noise to disturb me. The water brings me to the semi-dreaming state I wish could stretch through all my waking hours.

As I swim up for air and inhale a deep breath, reality crashes in. The large clock on the wall of the almost empty place tells me it's almost 11am and I have to go back home soon. Kimberly and Mum are waiting and despite everything, I am excited about this trip, and my first time at the beach.

I wrap myself in a towel, shower, change, then return home. A content smile stretches on my lips. I am so glad I had time for a quick water meditation after my last class before Spring Break. In a few months, my college freshman year will be over.

With rushed steps, I arrive at our small house in no time, greeted by my sister's snarky words.

"Let's go, Samantha. We can't leave Wyatt waiting. He is the only good thing that's happened in our life in the last decade and you seem intent on ruining it for us again."

I don't mind when Kimberly snaps at me, maybe because I am used to it or not present enough to care. Once again, I am lost, humming the melody that flutters in my dreams.

Many people would rather live in a book, but I would live in a song. I wish this melody that already lives in me could blend with me and become one somehow.

"I just need a second," I reply over my shoulder, hurrying to my bedroom to grab my suitcase, ready to spend the next two weeks in Wyatt's beach house.

I hope Kimberly is right about Mum's new boyfriend. I hope this one isn't like Mum's dozens of relationships since my father left when I was little. Wyatt seems like a decent guy, but I know Kimberly doesn't like him because of his personality. She is fond of his wealth.

As I make my way down to our open kitchen, Mum and Kimberly turn to look at me. My sister shakes her head, scrunching her nose, while Mum returns to what she was doing.

I look down at my leggings and white tank top, a contrast to Kimberly's glittering blue denim, plaid pink T-shirt, and leather boots combo.

"Sometimes I can't believe we are related." Kimberly frowns, judging my clothing choice.

"Girls, stop fighting!" Mum throws the words from the back of the kitchen counter, while packing some snacks for the hours-long drive.

"Don't worry, we won't fight in front of Wyatt as long as Samantha doesn't provoke me," my older sister says.

It's not like I will waste time trying to engage my sister in an argument. There is no point. She always believes whatever her brain conjures up as truth. Putting my headphones on, I play the guitar solo from one of the kids I teach, Noah. He is only twelve but very talented, and his progress always puts a smile on my face.

My phone vibrates with a notification, and I open the bank app to see what it's about. The payment from Ballet Academia has already dropped and is more than I expected. I smile at the four-figure number on my screen. If I can get a few more students for my private guitar classes or instruct one more children's ballet class, I will be able to move to a dorm at university and still support Mum with the rent. I've been saving for quite some time, and I am almost there, so close to achieving my goal for the last five years. I've been working on it since I started offering guitar lessons to the kids in the neighbourhood at the age of fourteen.

Once I have the money, I will move to the dorm where my best friend, Olivia, lives. There, I can spend my days the way I love, between dance classes, the swimming pool, and the aerial silks—free like a bird. A bird with her earphones plugged in as music embraces her with rhythm and harmony.

The honk of a car signals that Wyatt has arrived, and Kimberly rushes me. "Come on, get out of your head, weirdo. Don't make him wait."

"Girls, stop it!" Mum frowns at both of us.

Sighing, I follow them outside. Kimberly takes her time admiring Wyatt's red sports car as Mum drops her suitcase by the trunk and hurries to hug him. My eyes are trained on Mum's

3

smiling face, and I am relieved to see her this happy. She… we have been through a lot in the last few years.

I shake off my thoughts as Wyatt steps closer. Adjusting his cowboy hat, he eyes the two bags in my hands. "Hello, Sam. Do you want help with your suitcase?"

"Hello, Wyatt. No, it's fine." I smile back, placing my suitcases and Mum's in the spacious trunk as she plays with her phone without acknowledging our conversation.

She isn't a bad mother, but she never saw me. Not even for a second of my life. No one in Cedar Hill but my friend, Olivia, has ever seen me. It bothered me, but now I've gotten used to being invisible.

Have you ever felt you never belonged? From time to time, I can't stop wondering if everything around me is wrong or if I am the wrong one.

I hum at the infinity of water in front of me. The ebb and flow of the waves wash over me with longing. Following the sweet symphony, I set my feet into the water. Suddenly, I feel arms around me.

I look over my shoulder, but I can't see anyone. Yet this impossibility doesn't scare me. He is there. I know it without needing to see him.

It's as if I am in love with a ghost, a memory. Except I know better. He is not in my past. He is my future.

Warmth spreads across my cheek from his delicate kiss, and I want more. I crave him.

"You are finally here." His voice blows in my ear, distant and fleeting, like the final echo of the wind.

"I've been looking for you," I say, reaching for his invisible hands but only feeling water under my fingertips.

Have I? I don't know why I said those words, but I know they aren't a lie. They were a secret I had yet to tell myself.

"And I've been waiting, beloved." His husky voice pebbles goosebumps across my skin.

Like the soft touch of the water, his hands run down to my waist, and a soft moan escapes me.

"Jesus Christ, Samantha! Now you're moaning like a porn star?"

With a start, I wake up at Kimberly's words, bringing a hand to my chest.

"We are almost there," Wyatt announces, smiling at my mum as he tries to break the tension in the car.

I rub the sleepiness from my bleary eyes and look out the window. Bright joy radiates in my chest as my eyes find the sea. It's incredible, just like in my dream.

With a long sigh, I recall his touch and his voice. That was a strange dream. I've often dreamed about the song but never about anything else. So why does his voice sound so familiar, as if it's meant to complement the music, adding a bass note?

"Samantha, you won't scare Wyatt away like you did Denis!" Kimberly grits out in an angry whisper. Denis, one of Mum's ex-boyfriends, is the root of all my problems with Kimberly—she always reminds me of it.

"I didn't scare him away." I shake my head.

"No, you did worse!"

I should be over all this nagging and give it the importance it has, none. I am over it most of the time, but today I feel a little different, as if my emotions are bubbling to the surface.

After what felt like an hour, Wyatt parks by a large white house surrounded by manicured bushes and an ample porch.

The sea breeze invades my lungs the instant I open the car door, and I am lost to the world. I have to make a great effort to focus on reality and settle my suitcases in the guest room before I can ignore everything else, give in to the yearning in my chest, and dart to the empty beach. After I kick off my shoes, my bare feet soak in the gritty, lingering warmth of the sand, bringing me closer to the water.

A giggle of joy leaves me as the cool water touches my skin. I follow the ebbing waves, chasing this feeling as I hop around in the shallow waters. As I gaze at the boundless blue in front of me gilded by the orange beams of the setting sun, my heart tugs, and I walk in deeper until the water reaches my waist.

Tingles spark across my skin and I stop for a moment, taking all the blissful sensations in. I may be losing my mind. Maybe I am finally lucid. All I know is that the ever-present song in my mind is no longer a whisper. It is loud and clear, drawing my soul to the sea. It's like a call from home, so close I can touch it.

I can't help it. I can't deny it. I have to drown in it.

Dancing with myself in a free way I would never do in any class of my major, I spin my arms around my body. My giggles and laughter join the imaginary symphony as I swirl around.

When my back faces the ocean, a prickling sensation rises across my neck, and I can't brush off the feeling that I am being watched. I whirl around, scanning the deep waters, but I can't find anyone. Yet the weight of their eyes on me is undeniable. Someone isn't only looking at me but seeing within my soul and into my secrets. As if I am truly being seen for the first time in my life.

I turn to look in another direction to conclude that there is no one there, just the infinitude of the sea, my imagination, and the inaudible song strumming at my heartstrings as if they were a guitar.

CHAPTER 2
Collins

"I cannot believe there is yet another sharkman brawl in your territory. These boys are going bonkers, exuding testosterone and big-fish attitude waiting to be tamed," Melise says, looking at the semi-destroyed bar before her gaze settles on the wounded tail of one of the sharkmen in question.

Fortunately, we separated the fight before it escalated into a significant conflict. The fact that today's brawl occurred so close to the portal separating the Seven Seas' Queendom and the surface is yet another issue to be addressed. And since it happened in the Northern Atlantic Sea, I had to be the one to solve it. Of course, Melise could aid me as the high queen. Yet she has more pressing duties to deal with.

"Collins, my dear. I wonder why your territory has had the most conflicts lately. You know what they say, each guardian's domain is a reflection in and of themselves. Perhaps you are growing even more restless and troubled in the last few months. You should follow my lead and get yourself a lovely harem, or at least take a lover for a night." Concern vibrates in my sister's words.

I am aware she has good intentions, yet they are of no help. Having a harem or a one-night stand would not benefit me. Once one experiences the unique connection one has with a soulmate, a beloved, the embrace of a mere lover would be bereft of meaning and tangible pleasure.

"I am as well as I have been in the last couple of decades." I dismiss her.

"Hence not well at all—"

"You do not have to worry about me," I cut her off.

"Very well. You will find your way through once you are ready." Shrugging, Melise swims closer to the weaker merman.

With narrowed eyes, I shake my head, watching their exchange and how she volunteers to tame the shark-boy's big-fish attitude, as she put it. The guy will surely end up in my sister's royal harem by the end of the day.

Adjusting her hair to prevent it from falling onto the pearly tiara etched upon her forehead, she giggles. She places a hand on the sharkman's shoulder, the pearl embedded under his wrist shining at the contact, a sign of his arousal—something I don't want to see.

All merpeople have a pearl within their skin, for that is the vessel of our souls. Melise's pearl rests on her forehead, surrounded by the tiara engraved on her skin. Like the other six guardians, my pearl sits upon my collarbone. The common folk's pearl resides on their wrists, surrounded by a naturally inked bracelet.

Melise releases another lively laugh, wrapping her arms around the sharkman. My sister knows no bounds or bereavements, and from time to time, I envy her carefree spirit and uncanny ability to revel in every little encounter and event. Unlike me, she doesn't carry a past filled with harrowing grief. She has never met her soulmate—her beloved—just to lose them.

I still listen to the echoes of my beloved's soul song, caressing my own. Merfolk's souls are songs, a melody within to broadcast to our soulmate. Once one meets their beloved, their soul song blends with ours and their music fills the silence, converting life into a vivid symphony. Yet Sadb died, and the lingering notes of her melody became grief.

Unwilling to witness Melise's seduction game, I flutter my tail to leave. But an odd craving wraps across my chest once I am a short distance away. I am compelled to dash to the surface as if something is calling for me. Exhaling a lungful of water, I attempt to ignore the call and swim in the opposite direction. I have not felt such a yearning since Sadb passed away. Yet the ache grows strong, spanning from my chest to my guts, and I am powerless against it.

Cursing under my breath, I edge towards the sizeable, gated portal of the North Atlantic Sea, the magical portal separating my enclave and the world of terrestrials. The light surrounding it shines brighter as I approach, resonating with my energy. Crossing through, I leave our queendom and swim to the surface. As I reach closer to shore, I am drawn to a presence, a sweet and quiet song blooming from the shallow waters. I halt as my eyes fix on *her*. A petite human giggles, swirling in the water as the sea breeze blows her almost white-blonde hair. The sound is ethereal and mellifluous as it washes over me with a striking sense of déjà vu. I disregard the absurd thought, for no one can be like my Sadb. Every creature in the sea has one, and only one, soulmate. To that, there is no parallel.

This human is not my beloved.

She cannot be my beloved.

Years of grief and solitude are affecting my mind, creating a vision over the waters.

I must leave this girl and this illusion behind. Perhaps this is a sign that my sister is right and I am indeed more troubled, or rather, losing my sanity.

I close my eyes, yet to no avail. Her presence is intoxicating and unavoidable, demanding my single-minded focus. My gaze sails from her delicate nose to the swell of her breasts, marvelling at how the sunbeams reflect on her foam-white skin. She smiles to herself, moving with a grace rarely found in any creature from above the sea. The little human is beautiful and so full of life that she awakes a dormant part of my heart.

Once she strides closer, my heart hammers in my chest, and the pearl in the dip between my collarbone throbs. My soul song hits a crescendo as if longing to reach her song and entwine in a sensual symphony. I shift my weight as my cock pokes at the inner part of my tail, ready to thrust into her. How good she would feel in my embrace as my hands run down her skin, fingers entangling in her blonde locks.

I want her like I haven't wanted anyone in decades, since … Shaking my tail, I fight back the thought.

Blazing maelstrom!

A single sight of her enchants my full attention once again. But it is only when she prances in the shallow water, and I catch sight of the green of her eyes, that the sea tilts on its axis.

Mine! Recognition strikes me like lightning, and my body quivers, muscles going stiff.

It cannot be! There is not, nor has there ever been, such a thing as a second-chance beloved. This is impossibly wrong.

The Sea Gods must have mistakenly connected our souls.

Regardless of the yearning searing through my flesh and thundering my soul song with the highest note, I cannot want this woman.

She glances in my direction, but before she can see me, I swim into the depths of my world, reaching for the gate of the North Atlantic Sea to leave this mistake behind. I will not replace my Sadb or betray her memory by gazing or smiling at any other woman. This tantalising song shall be smothered into silence.

To my disbelief, Melise is waiting for me by the gate with a grin. "Were you idling on the surface? I thought I would never see the day … again. You look like someone who just saw a ghost fish. Did something happen?" she asks, swimming so close to me that our tails touch. Her tail changes to bright purple, indicating curiosity.

"Nothing happened, Melly. Let's go home," I bark as I swim away.

I did not see a ghost, but the spectre of a future that shall never belong to me. The beautiful little human is better forgotten.

CHAPTER 3
Samantha

After a long swim, I return to the sand to take a nap. The dreams about that invisible man holding me in his arms and running his hands down my body didn't allow me to sleep well.

I awake as the sun sets, the beach is empty, and I enjoy the quietness. At least now I don't have to worry about going from a ghost to a crab under the scorching Texas sun.

As I reach for the water bottle in my bag, I notice my phone's screen flashing. Olivia's message is popping up.

> Olie 🐾: How is your first day on the beach? ☺

> ME: Great! Mum and Kimberly went on a shopping spree, so I am relaxing alone. How is your trip going?

She tells me about her time in Mexico with her boyfriend and his family, before commenting on Wyatt.

> Olie 🐎: I hope Wyatt is not a douche or an alcoholic like your mum's boyfriend number 15. LOL.

Olivia kept score on Mum's relationships; though she is concerned about my mother, she especially worries about me. But I am not troubled this time. Wyatt seems harmless.

> ME: He is a nice guy, and Mum is happy.

> Olie 🐎: I hope he is nice enough to have your mum moving in with him or pay for her rent, so you can be free from the burden."

I laugh at her words and how straight to the point she is. Olivia's no-nonsense words from the day she found out I helped my mum to pay most of the rent play in my mind. *"Why do you even pay for your mum's rent when she doesn't give a flying shit about you?"*

Olie doesn't understand how Mum had struggled to raise Kimberly and me with no support, and now that I have a way to do it, it's my turn to give something back. It feels like the right thing to do, especially when Mum is still so entangled in her unsuccessful romantic relationships, always reduced to shreds

13

when yet another boyfriend leaves her. I try to be her harbour and stone when I know everything else may come down to a whirlwind of loss later.

ME: I hope Mum takes things slowly this time ☺.

With a shake of my head, I put the phone back in my bag and stretch before heading to the water.

As I swim deeper, I hear a female voice calling me. I stop to look around and try to see who is calling.

"Here, my dear," she says, and I spot her in the depths before she reaches closer.

I blink, surprised at how gorgeous the pinky-purple-haired woman is, especially when my eyes settle on the pearl tiara tattooed on her forehead.

When she is close enough, she says, "I am Melise."

"I am Samantha. Nice to meet you." I conceal my frown of confusion. Who is she, and why haven't I seen her on the beach?

"It might sound strange, but I want you to meet someone." She beams, taking my hand in hers.

"What?"

She doesn't reply, only drags me down under the water. Instinct kicks in, and I push her away, trying to free myself from her grip and return to the surface to breathe.

What the hell is she doing?

Despite the sting, I force my eyes open underwater. Looking down, I see a vast and stunning pink fluttering fish.

Wait, that's not a fish! It's her tail?! I've never seen such a perfect mermaid costume, and of its own accord my hand reaches out to touch it. Instead of latex, I feel scales.

My God, it's real!

The realisation shocks and soothes me in a way I can't understand.

Gasping in surprise, I swallow water, and my lungs burn, renewing my desire to return to the surface. But Melise only ushers me further down, showing me a small cylindrical shell and motioning to my mouth. I must be out of my mind because I do as she signals. As I place the shell close to my lips, it releases a sweet liquid that I swallow. I cough for air, only to realise that I can suddenly breathe. Recovering my wits, I try to process how insane all of this is.

"Dear, don't fight it, just breathe," she coos, placing a hand on my shoulder to steady me.

"How can I hear you underwater?" I ask, realising I can hear myself as well.

"With the magic in the shell-nut's help. I apologise for my lack of manners, but it has been quite some time since I have spirited away a human. I must say, you are far braver than the sailors I've once played with."

"Sailors?" I echo, confused. I blink a few times, noticing that the salt water no longer stings my eyes.

"They were fine. I would never take someone to my queendom against their will. We just had some fun, and I left them on the shore, believing it was nothing but a dream. Now, now, come with me," she beams, guiding me further down until we see a purple-blue gate gleaming with light.

To my disbelief, I am not scared, only a little confused. So, following my instincts as if I had done it many times, I swim along, crossing the portal and arriving at a large circular room filled with gates like the one we passed through.

My body isn't pulled up any longer. I can step on the stone ground with ease. The water here feels different… lighter. That's the word I am looking for. I blink, noticing that the colours grew more vibrant after we crossed the passage.

On the ceiling, colourful starfishes dance in circles, surrounded by glowing jellyfish swirling with magical delicacy as though they were part of the water.

"How is this possible?" I ask, lost in wonder as my gaze roams around the place until it finds a grinning Melise.

"What? The synchronised dance? They do it only when we have visitors. Starfish are skilful show-offs."

"I mean, everything here, you, this place?" I ask, unable to stop looking around and taking in every astonishing detail.

Carefree schools of fish parade around us, crossing the gaps between the pillars at the bottom of the room. Is this place a hall? "Where are we?" I add.

"We are in The Queendom of the Seven Seas, Tal Lashar." She taps her chin, her now bright golden tail swishing in circles. "How can I answer your other questions? Humans tend to believe nothing is beyond them, no creatures, nor magic. This way, they keep a blind eye to all the enchantments and blessings surrounding their lives. Although it changes constantly, Tal Lashar is as old as the world. Long story short, our people descend from Tritons," she explains.

That is a sound explanation, and although I know I should be shocked and maybe terrified, something in me easily accepts her words. The sense of familiarity lessens my shock at the impossible and incredible underwater queendom. Maybe it's because I've always hoped for a world with magic growing up in a hard reality.

And this place feels less strange than Kimberly's coveted rodeos or country parties. Unable to shake off the sensation that this place isn't as odd to me as it's supposed to be, I ask, "Have I been here before, and like your sailors, I thought it was only a dream?"

Melise lets out the most beautiful musical laugh. "I don't believe so, my dear. Can you feel it?"

I nod. I can feel it, although I don't exactly know what it is.

I look at her beautiful shimmering tail again, and the fact that I've eaten fish nuggets for lunch strikes me with guilt. Shaking my head, I try to think about something else.

"Who do you want me to meet?" I ask, recalling what she said when we met.

"I believe you are someone important to my brother, thus I will be delighted for you to meet him. Come with me, the essential cannot be explained with words."

With an encouraging smile, she ushers me into a long corridor. The song in my mind grows louder, reaching a beautiful crescendo before dropping into a lower note of longing. It has never sounded this intoxicating, transporting me into deeper waters and hauling me ahead as if I were wrapped with its strings. I can't help but walk towards it as every note drives me into a more profound trance.

Wait, I can hear it loud and clear. The music is not in my mind anymore. It surrounds me like an aquatic blanket.

The more I see, the more I feel like I know these waters. I smile as my heart syncs with the beat, washing me over with the certainty that this place feels like home, as though, for the first time in forever, I am where I *belong*.

Melise and I enter another large room, where we come across a dark-blue-tailed merman. When he turns around, I freeze, absent from everything but the soaring song and the frantic rhythm of my heart. That's the man from my dreams! He... he is the song!

"Samantha, my dear, this is my brother, Collins," Melise says, but I don't look at her. I can't take my eyes off him, afraid that the song will stop and I will wake up to yet another dream. I hope to at least get to the moaning part before this time. My skin is tingling to feel his touch.

Collins narrows his eyes at me, locking his jaw.

"Why did you do it, Melise?"

My gaze slides from his blue eyes with purple flecks to his strong squared jaw and the dark shoulder-length hair framing his

17

stunning face. Like Melise, he has a pearl tattooed, but this one is on his collarbone rather than the forehead. The sight of his muscular, tanned chest and bulky arms sends moisture pooling between my thighs. Lighter blue fins adorn the sides of his large dark-blue tail, as thick as two legs placed together. I don't want to stare, but as if I am compelled by magic, I can't help myself.

I am so lost in the cadence of his voice that I can hardly process his words, only the strong bass carrying them. I want him to speak more, anything, everything, even if it is not directed at me.

"You had no right to meddle, Melise!"

"Stop it now, Collins. You will startle the little human. And for Poseidon's sake, don't be as hard-headed as the carapace of a lobster. If you'd only listen."

"No!"

The song stretching across my mind muffles all the words, and of their own accord, my legs move closer to the gorgeous merman.

"A few minutes. Just talk to her. Deep inside this carapace, you know I am right and bright." Melise says something about carapaces I can't fully acknowledge. Intoxicated by the song and his presence, I outstretch my hand, and as I reach his shoulder, he abruptly pulls away.

"Get away from here and never come back! You do *not belong* here!" he thunders, bringing me tumbling back to reality.

"What?" I ask as I start processing his words. He doesn't want me here? Can he feel this? Whatever this is—a connection, chemistry, magic?

"Have you not heard me? This is not your place. Return to your shore. I do not want you," he bellows.

My heart sinks, and pain radiates across my chest.

With his cold angry instance, he proceeds, "You—"

"I hear you. You don't have to repeat yourself. I am leaving!" A burst of rage like I've never experienced flares in my words. Kicking the water as quickly as possible, I swim down the hall.

"Go after her!" Frustration is evident in Melise's tone.

18

"No!" he affirms.

Their voices grow quieter, fading when I enter the large hall of shimmering gates. After looking between the seven of them for a moment, I realise that Melise and I came from the purple-blue one—the same shade as his eyes. I hope it means this is the right door.

Opening it, I rush to the surface, and struggle to breathe when I'm only a few feet away. My lungs burn, desperate for air but only able to inhale water. Melise's magic must have worn off. Speeding up, I break through, and my head rises above the water to take in a lungful of air.

Disoriented, I take a while to find my way towards the beach. Heading to the shore, his words sear through me again. *"You do not belong."* How foolish I am to believe that this magical sea realm was my place. There is no place for me!

Tears roll down my cheeks as I push faster, ignoring my aching muscles but not managing to do the same with my broken heart. Why does it hurt so much? It isn't supposed to be so bad. I don't even know that man. Except, I do, from my silly dreams and a deeper place inside that I would rather cut off.

A large wave crashes over me, plunging me down as the seawater swallows me whole, dragging me around with brutal force. Fluttering my arms and legs, I swim upwards, coughing up water. My eyes and throat sting, but I keep my head above, fighting the tide to get to the shore.

I lick my lips, taking a stuttering breath as his image consumes my mind again. I am haunted by his face, the song, and the tingling in the bottom of my stomach. Anger floods me—I hate being unable to control or understand these feelings and help myself as they drown me. Stupid merman and his beautiful eyes!

As if the sea can hear me and decides to laugh at my expense, another gigantic wave plummets me further down, too far from the surface. With long flails of my arms, I try to pull up, but I only manage to move a couple inches, swallowing too much water. I clench my eyes shut to shield them from the salty sting and force myself to move faster, legs kicking harder.

I am too exhausted. I can't do this for much longer. I just want to breathe.

Suddenly, the song rises, and strong arms envelop me, pushing my head through the surface. I spurt heaps of water, trying to inhale, but mostly choking.

He holds me tighter, the feeling of sparks of electricity rising on my skin at our contact.

His large palm presses against my chest, coaxing me to gush out more water.

My mind reels.

The song.

His warmth.

Him.

Collins.

My exhausted body is close to giving up, only soaking in the delicious tingles spreading across it. It's almost soothing, yet it isn't. Collins has just rejected me.

I toss in his arms, half lost to the haze in my mind. I have to flee his embrace before I sink into it. He tightens his hold on me, stilling my squirms.

So good. No, it's not supposed to be that good!

I attempt to cry out, but only water leaves my throat, and I spill some more. My feeble hands reach for his shoulder as he lifts me higher and presses my chest against his to help me cough out water.

As soon as I regain my breath, I protest in a croaky voice, "Let go of me."

"I cannot, little human, else you will drown." He cradles me against his chest, flaring a buzz of electricity down my spine.

Forcing my eyes open, I look around, only to realise we are close to the shore.

"I won't drown. Just let go of me. Don't touch me." I must be able to reach the ground now and make my way to the beach with slow steps.

Instead, he gently places me on a solid, rough surface. His eyes linger on me as he studies me from head to toe, and as soon as he is satisfied, he swims away.

I heave a sigh of relief. Collins' presence suffocated me as much as the chastising waves. And I didn't know what to do with his inexplicable pull on me. *But now he is gone, it's over.*

Minding the rough edges of the rock I am on, I sit up, and after filling my lungs with air, I walk to the beach without looking back.

Arriving at Wyatt's house, I take a quick shower and change before I collect my suitcase to start packing. Although I don't understand and loathe this connection, being rejected by someone I care so deeply about flipped a switch inside me. I didn't miss the irony that it took me to swim under the sea to take my head from under the water and see with clarity.

My blood still boils, and my heart thunders in my chest as I ride the storm of rage, something I've never experienced. But if there is something Collins' aggressive rejection showed me is that I don't wish to waste a moment longer in a place I am not really wanted. So, without care, I shove the rest of my clothes in the suitcase and place my knee on top to force the loaded bag to close.

Then I march to the living room as all the anger I didn't allow myself to feel for my whole life strikes with a vengeance. Being booted by the literal man of my dreams – or better said, tailed by the merman of my song – filled my shunned cup, putting things into perspective. As much as I won't tolerate his monumental burn, I won't put up with the little flares from the things I didn't really care as much about.

There, I come across Mum and Kimberly. Mum places two pasta bowls on a tray as my sister plays with her phone, probably working on her YouTube channel.

21

"Mum, I am leaving earlier. I have plenty to do back in Cedar Hill." I would use the time in my favour to make enough money and be able to move to the dorm before Mum and Kimberly return to our house.

I won't try to conform to somewhere I don't belong anymore but work on creating a place I can call home and a life that fits me. God! It took a broken heart and a terrifying experience to figure that out. Better late than never.

"Sure, Sam. Water the plants when you are there," Mum says with a nod as she rushes upstairs carrying the food tray. Her reaction is nothing out of the ordinary, entirely expected.

I am about to open the door when Kimberly's angry words have me turning around.

"What now, Samantha? Do you want attention like on the day you told Mum about Denis and me? Stop annoying us. You won't get attention. You ruined everything for Mum and me. Dad left because he didn't want another child and it was too late to get a stupid abortion. We never wanted you! You were just a weird alien in our lives, an odd duck fucking up everything! No one ever wanted you!"

"I don't care, Kimberly. I want myself! I want my life and that's enough."

It wasn't the first time Kimberly told me how I ruined our mother's life and how she unsuccessfully tried to abort me. Last time, she even claimed that Mum's frustrated attempts to get rid of me affected my brain, which was why everything was wrong with me. I didn't use to care. I was lost in my head and daydreams, not present enough to bother. But now I had enough. I have had enough of being rejected and unwanted. Hell! I won't allow myself to feel wrong and inappropriate in a family and a place I know in my gut I've never belonged to. I don't want to be part of their dysfunctional family. My only concern is to make sure Mum is okay, and no other boyfriend hurts her.

I can't deny I want *him,* but it doesn't matter. Now I just have to want myself hard enough to pull out of this hole and claim every second of my life.

"What the hell? You are so fucking odd, Samantha!" Kimberly frowns, taking a step back.

I don't bother to reply, only leave the house. It isn't as though I've asked Kimberly to drive me to the bus station. I can walk there. An hour's walk will help me to clear my mind.

With rushed strides, I move ahead. Putting my headphones on, I set the music as loud as possible so that I can attempt to silence his song. Like a curse, it follows me around, sending me back to the depths of the sea. But I refuse to break again, not for him or anyone else.

Arriving at the bus station, I check its website. Great, I have to wait for two hours. I take a calming breath, trying to see the bright side. I will be away from him soon, be able to speed up my moving-out plan, and tomorrow I will do one of the things I love the most—dangle in my aerial silk.

A message from my sister pops up on my phone, but I leave it unread. I have done everything independently for the last few years, and it isn't different now, only a little more obvious, which is freeing. Who could say it took me almost drowning to take the first deep breath in years? Yet another text pops up, and I pocket my phone.

I scoff, recalling Kimberly's words and what happened to Denis. My sister hates me because when I was fourteen, and she was almost sixteen, I caught her and Mum's ex, Denis, making out in the kitchen. I knew he was yet another predator. There is no lost love between a fifteen-year-old and her stepdad. So, I told Mum Denis was flirting with Kimberly, without saying it was mutual, not to throw her under the bus. Mum broke up with him, and since then, my sister has punished me for shooing away the love of her life.

Maybe Kimberly, Mum and I have in common our uncanny ability to drive people—and fish people—away.

Collins' image surges in my mind, and I can't shake it off. My exhausted eyes close of their own accord, giving in to his frown, his handsome face, and those muscular arms around me, sending magical jolts across my body. His thick tail! And I can't stop the thought—does he have a dick hidden there?

Shaking my head, I huff at myself. It's not like I will ever meet his shaft or come across the absence of it. My life will stay under a non-dick policy. After seeing what my mum went through for years, I'm convinced that most dick owners are dicks themselves, real jerks.

CHAPTER 4
Collins

I turn and toss in my shell bed, unable to fall asleep. For the second night in a row, I could not catch a minute of rest. I've spent the last day and a half trying to forget her, but the harder I try to forget, the more her image and song permeate my mind.

Covering my face with a soft seaweed pillow, I try to fall asleep once more. However, when I close my eyes, I can only see her round green eyes brimming with terror whilst she almost drowned.

After the little human left, I felt her distress, screams of agony permeating her song. Without hesitating, I went after her. Witnessing her struggle and how she tried to pull away from me, although I was the only pillar between her and the fury of the waves, plummeted me into guilt.

Once again, I curse myself under my breath. It is my fault, another indication that it is wise for both of our sakes to keep my distance.

"Allow me to forget you, little human," I murmur into the dark bedroom. Yet the sweet and tantalising song from her soul only rises higher.

Her soul song is beautiful and harrowingly, similar to the music my dead beloved's soul exuded. A soul song is the most intimate of melodies. One only our beloved can fully listen to, and once the tune first enters the shells of our ears, it lingers, worming into our hearts and making its home there. The human's song will haunt me until the day I die, and I cannot help but smile at this thought.

Rising, I frown at myself for my drifting thoughts and focus on remembering every soft note of my Sadb's song. I cannot allow the girl's song to bewitch me, etch itself into my mind and replace the only treasure I have left of Sadb—our connection, the melodic flutter of her life.

"Damnation!" My hands rub at my face as I fight the echo of her music and the unwelcome pull the human has on me.

Giving up on sleep, I leave my palace wing to swim about. When I was younger, race-swimming or even a swim-stroll soothed me. Lately, it does not seem to help much, yet I am out of options, for I know nothing in the Seven Seas and Earth alike can ease the weight that plummets into my chest like an old ship anchor.

Have I made the right decision or acted on impulse? Perhaps Melise is right, and I am becoming a grumpy fish, unable to curb my rage and the rash outburst of emotions I've worked hard to bury into oblivion. This anger should be directed at anyone but the delicate human.

With my face sunk in my hands, I bellow in frustration, "Maelstrom blazes!" I should not have yelled at her and shattered the gleam I recognised in her eyes, bond induced or not.

Flailing my tail, I swim at high speed despite the fact racing will not dwindle the reeling in my mind.

Once the light from the surface is filtering through the water, announcing the new day, I come across Melise in the coral garden surrounding the palace. My sister wears a mask of worry on her face, her usual jovial expression marred by a frown as her light eyes narrow at me.

"Why did you do that?" she asks, edging closer with a few powerful flails of her now grey tail, a token of her poor mood.

I know very well what she is asking about, the little human.

"I do not want another beloved. I cannot betray Sadb's memory. This is an anomaly, something that is not supposed to occur. Everyone has a single beloved, only one soul song that harmonises with their own. Second chances are not supposed to exist!" I rant.

"It's not an oddity, but rather a miracle. Stop finding excuses. Sadb would like you to pursue your happiness, and you are aware of that. I know you well, Collins. The loyalty to Sadb's memory is not the main reason, for there is no chance of you forgetting her and the soul-singing life you created together. Now spill it like a squid spurts their ink!"

"That is the only reason." I grimace.

Can she not simply drop the matter?

"You can fool yourself; however, you cannot fool me. Why did you reject that sweet little human?"

"Because of *that*! She is a sweet little human, petite, hence fragile. I cannot lose another beloved, Melise. I cannot deal with such agony and this feeble human is there only to be lost. She is dainty as a starfish, and in the few hours I have known her, she has almost lost her life."

"Because of you, jellyfish-brained man! She almost died due to *your* fear. Now fin up, and act on your trepidation. If you cannot lose another beloved, work on not losing Samantha. Ensure she will live healthy and well."

Samantha. So that is the human's name. With all the chaos raging on yesterday, I missed noticing it spoken. The mellifluous name suits her.

As I am about to leave, Melise's words give me pause. "Stop sabotaging your own happiness. Sadb's death and the loss of your daughter were not your fault. We welcomed my dearest niece back into our lives a couple of years ago. Now you have been awarded with yet another blessing. Embrace it, and when you see the girl, start grovelling for the sake of all Gods under and over the seas. She has no reason to forgive your ill behaviour and grant you another chance, so you had better give her plenty of reasons for that. Remember, humans are not used to merfolk's intense emotions, or she will think you are over the top."

How I hate my sister's meddling habit. Beyond that, I hate that once again she is right.

I shake my head but must concede. "Thank you, Melly."

Raising her brows, she graces me with a humourless grin. "I am always here for you, even when you are not here for yourself. Now, rush and go find your lovely human."

I must make sure she is at least well. That is a sound plan. I will watch her from a distance to see for her safety.

I nod, focusing on Samantha's song. The notes are muffled by distance, indicating she is no longer near the beach. Yet regardless of her whereabouts, the music of her soul will always lead me to her. Without wasting time, I dart to the concoction shop to gather what I need.

While I cross the town with powerful flails, an echo of Samantha's song brims my mind. Her music, eyes, and every glorious inch of her skin captivated me. There is no denial. I will not be able to forget her face, and the melody of her soul will not stop entwining with my own.

Setting my tail on a stone, I attempt to filter only her location and ignore the ocean of sensations her song entails.

Just find her, ensure her drowning did not cause a severe injury, and leave. A task I am capable of completing without error, I assure myself.

Melise's words ricochet in my ears. I am allowing fear to guide me; I am a coward. Yet no one who has not lost their beloved, the other half of their soul, can understand my grief. The agony is so intense that most merfolk do not survive losing their soulmates.

I have survived, and I do not regret that—for even the harrowing pain and soul-consuming solitude were worth it once I

28

was reunited with my daughter. However, it did not mean I would risk venturing through the dry abyss of hell again. No fish would, not even a brainless jellyfish.

I exhale a stream of bubbles. I will not be able to survive this again. No one should; it is even more abnormal than being granted a second chance beloved.

One more key of her song enters my ears, possessing yet another piece of my soul. This particular note is dipped in melancholy, and the pearl in the centre of my collarbone, the vessel of my soul song, tugs painfully. The tone dawns on me with realisation. There is something I dread more than losing her, namely her suffering and pain. Despite myself and all the misery I can harbour, even if it means submitting my tail to more grief, I cannot allow her to suffer. I must remedy it.

As I frantically run my fingers through my hair, I pace about, my tail sweeping against the ground.

Only ensuring her safety will not suffice! She needs more, and so do I.

Despite what I have been telling myself, renouncing my happiness will not benefit either of us. I refuse to further hurt my beloved due to my consternation. I have already done enough in this regard. Samantha has felt the bond, which will linger in her soul; thus, she too will experience the sorrow our parting will bring about. That is not something I wish for the peskiest sharkman-brawl-riser, let alone for the sweet human singing in my awakened nights.

A bond that is supposed to be a rare encounter of songs composed by the Gods now harms Samantha.

Instead, I must show her the beauty the connection between beloveds arouses. I must find her and do what my meddlesome sister suggested, gain her trust even if only to be able to bring her joy. My pearl pulses at the thought, and this decision alone is enough to bask my soul with a long-forgotten sense of peace.

Besides, I shall show her beyond the alluring bond between us. I want Samantha to know me, to choose me. For that, I must earn both her trust and the opportunity to court her.

I only hope it will work. Dealing with another loss might be more than I can take.

Entering the concoction shop, I rake my eyes over the wall of drawers loaded with various potions and elixirs any sea creature may need.

With graceful movements no legged creature can muster, the owner of the shop swims close, brushing her flowing blue hair behind her ears. Zoe is a rare sea nymph and the only being in the Tal Lashar to trade and collect an ample variety of concoctions created by different creatures, from witches to fae.

"Welcome, Guardian Collins. Do you need yet another potion to enable you to breathe on the land?" she asks, motioning to the spot on the drawers where the concoction lays.

I pause to think about her question as I survey the drawers once more. I have not visited the surface lands often, except after I found my hybrid daughter—the only gem I have left of my Sadb. On the frequent occasions we visited her, Melise and I benefited from both the potion to breathe on the surface and a floating bubble wrapped around our tails that permitted mobility.

However, Samantha is human, and such an approach will not be effective. I cannot swim forward into her life and distress her again with a world foreign to her. To smooth my way towards her heart, I need something more human, more familiar to Samantha.

I hiss out a breath, forcing bubbles to stream from my nostrils. Samantha was so brave to follow Melise into an unknown realm, only to be cruelly rejected and shoved away. Under my breath, I curse at myself, casting my gaze down. That's when my eyes zero in on the fluttering legs of the nymph.

"Yes, but with that, I need a potion that gives me legs."

Zoe's almond-shaped dark eyes widen, but she nods, fetching a small bottle from the top drawer. "I have something. It's a new

30

product, recently developed by the fae. As far as I know, it was only used a couple of times, and its efficacy is doubtful. I wouldn't recommend its unrestricted usage, at least not before it goes through another round of tests. The Fae Ministry isn't fully aware of the side effects of any dosage surpassing a droplet, which will only be effective for an hour."

The fae were quite ingenious with their crystals and concoctions, brewing potions to the advantage of the other species. However, one hour will not be enough time to right my wrongs.

"I will need far more than an hour." My voice vibrates with determination as I outstretch my hand to collect the concoction.

"Very well, Guardian. Please use it in moderation and stay alert for any side effects. If you feel unwell, stop with the usage immediately," she recommends, worry lacing her words.

Zoe is an old acquaintance. I have known her for at least a couple hundred years, and it is evident that she cares about me and my family.

"I will be careful."

I will not act like an irresponsible crustacean, yet I am willing to do whatever I have to do not to lose yet another beloved, not to lose *her.* And unfortunately, I need such appendages to help charm the little human.

After paying Zoe, I fetch what I need to succeed on the surface. One of my siblings is a collector, and she has as many human trinkets as one might imagine. Nori hoarded her goods, from plundering sank ships to sending crabs to snatch pieces of clothes while oblivious humans idle on the beach.

Once I have everything I need, I drink the fae potion and reach the surface, following Samantha's song like a beacon to guide me to a new home as a seafarer following the North Star.

It takes me a while once I am on the surface, but I finally find Samantha. At least it gave me enough time to get used to the land appendages, and now I can use the legs without making a fool of myself.

She is close, only a small distance away. Her song rises into a crescendo, vibrating with a flare of passion, but I do not miss the broken notes in between, charged with both hurt and bravery. Crossing the hall of a so-called gymnastic studio—whatever it might mean—I open the door to enter a large empty room. My eyes lock with Samantha's graceful form dangling over the ground. Without noticing me, she swirls her arms around a long patch of purple silk, climbing before flitting in the air as if the cloth were her wings.

I watch on with heated rapture, unable to pull my gaze from the dainty movements she creates with such ease, unwilling to interrupt this moment.

She is stunning.

She is flowing as if she were one with the air.

No gravity can halt her fluttering fluidly.

I am lost in her. Lost in this moment. Yet this transports me to another memory, a similar scene I witnessed decades ago. With an exhale, I dismiss those thoughts. I refuse to allow them to take me, for I am here for Samantha and only her.

Drawn to the sound of my rapid breathing, Samantha tilts her head in my direction. She gasps once her green eyes meet mine, losing her grip. Before I can reach her, she attempts to land; instead, she touches down awkwardly on her ankle with a yelp. Clenching her eyes, she braces herself for the full weight of her body to descend. Before her hands and knees can take the brunt of the fall, I reach her, wrap my arms around her, and pull her to my chest.

"Why are you here, Collins?" She narrows her eyes, escaping my grasp and crawling away as she bites her lip in a failed attempt to conceal a moan of pain.

CHAPTER 5
Samantha

I still can't shake off the surprise as I hobble away from him.

"Samantha." My name on his lips, vibrating in such a deep bass, sends a jolt of pleasure through my body. I stiffen at the sensation but soon collect myself and brush it off.

"Stop now! You don't get to reject me, kick me to the curb and then show up in my training to make me fall."

I stagger away, putting as much distance between us as possible until my sweaty back meets the cold surface of the wall. Adjusting against my newfound support, I glance in his direction.

Exhaling, he speaks cautiously as his eyes darken with an expression I can't read from here. "I'm sorry for making you lose your balance."

To my relief, he doesn't come near me, respecting my space. As my eyes roam the length of his body, I notice he has legs, and I have to contain a gasp.

Keeping my stance, I narrow my eyes at him. "What do you want?" The words are bitter on my tongue.

I cross my arms in front of me as if they could protect my heart. With him here, the song is so loud and clear that it eclipses everything else, reducing the world to the two of us.

After hauling an exhale, he starts, "I acknowledge that your indignation is righteous."

I ignore his *acknowledgment*, a burst of anger rising in my chest. "You were pretty clear in your words. You don't want me. I don't belong with you. You have no right to be here!"

"I understand. I apologise for how I reacted and for what you've experienced. I wish I could take back my words, but I cannot. However, I can do everything in my capability to atone for my mistakes."

I narrow my eyes. "Why do you think that *I* want you?"

God! I am lying to myself. I do want him. With him near, my blood is humming with pleasure and desire so strong that it makes me dizzy. I have to fight back and say *no* to him. He can't just come here and tear apart my determination. I've spent the last day nursing my broken heart and the agonising feeling of what could have been. And now that I am feeling well enough to defy gravity and hover in the air, he shows up, wanting to take his rejection back.

"At least let me take you to see a healer. Allow me to help you with that."

The music coming from him drops into a sombre note, and the room's temperature decreases. His deep sadness trickles into me as if it were my own. Am I falling for a mermaid song? Some kind of spell?

"Stay away."

From the corner of my eye, I see him flinching. A mask of regret stretched on his face as his eyes dull, growing dark like the abyss of the sea. I clench my eyes and try not to feel it, not to fall for him. After long minutes of a heavy and almost suffocating silence, I turn my face towards him.

My arms tighten around myself, and I nervously chew at my lip, but I decide to take a little leap of faith. I can't ignore my desire for the sake of being petty and stubborn. I have to be brave, even if it means ending up a little… broken. Hearing him out doesn't mean I will end up with my legs wrapped around him and his hands squeezing my heart, right?

"How can I trust you won't change your mind again? I don't want to be part of your game."

Despite the mesmerising connection humming between us, I refuse to engage in some kind of toxic dance. I've seen my mum doing that many times with her exes, giving them second chances only to have their behaviour improve for a couple of weeks before everything goes horribly wrong.

When I look back at him, Collins's gaze locks with mine, keeping me in a sort of trance.

"This is no game for me, Samantha. I regret how I initially reacted. Still, I would like the opportunity to explain. None of what I am about to say justifies my poor behaviour, but it might help you to understand it."

He pauses, almost as if he is expecting me to protest, but I don't say a word.

"My beloved—or soulmate, as many call it—perished over twenty years ago, and I never expected to find the same kind of connection again until I met you."

Without fully registering his words, my heart tugs at his loss, hurting for him as if it had happened to me.

Wait, what did he say I am to him?

"Soulmate?" I echo like a fool. Loosely collecting my bodily functions, I haphazardly slide down the wall until I settle on the ground in a more comfortable position that doesn't force weight on my ankle. I didn't have the chance to take a good look at it, but I think it's sprained. I only know that it hurts like hell.

My eyes meet his again as the word resonates in my mind like a song of its own. So that's why I feel this pull of an irresistible connection to him.

36

"Yes, that is what you are to me." He scuffs closer with measured steps.

I even got rejected by my own soulmate. The realisation rekindles the burn of his words. Without thinking, I shift to hug my legs, wincing as the pain from my ankle radiates through my leg.

"We have to take you to see a healer."

I sigh at his words. He has a good point, and a bag of ice won't be enough to reduce the swelling.

I don't reply, only shuffle away when he reaches to touch the non-swollen part of my leg.

"Samantha, I am aware I do not deserve your trust, and you have no reason to give it to me. However, I wish to dedicate my future to giving you those reasons. If you would grant me the opportunity, I would be honoured to court you." Hope gleams in his eyes, illuminating his handsome face as he waits for my response.

This isn't fair. Being that gorgeous should be illegal.

"Court me?"

He sounds like a Victorian character from a movie, but his words warm my chest. I look away, only breaking from his hypnotic gaze will I be able to think straight.

But my heart pounds so quickly that my thoughts dissolve into a foggy mist.

His proximity.

The dreams.

The music.

As if spellbound, I am enveloped by all the allure that draws me to him, and the fear pulsing in my veins and flooding my mind has no voice.

I want him. I want him more than I've wanted anything.

I close my eyes and take a calming breath, but it does nothing to appease my racing pulse. Facing him and hoping I won't regret it, I say, "Only one chance."

The shock leaves his face, replaced by a gorgeous smile that lights up his eyes, and he brings the back of my hand to his lips, kissing it.

Tingles radiate from the spot his lips touch and I swallow back a moan.

"Thank you, Samantha."

After standing up, he outstretches a hand to help me up and I hesitate before taking it. With a questioning look, he ghosts his arm around my waist, only wrapping it there to steady me once I nod my consent.

As we take a few steps forward, I wince, unable to keep the weight off my ankle. The swelling is increasing and walking isn't a good idea.

"May I carry you?" Collins offers.

"Yes."

He scoops me up in his arms, pressing me against his muscular chest, and I can't help but melt into his arms. I sigh in frustration, still angry but also curious about what courting means. Yet beyond anything, my mind swims in confusion.

After we went to the neighbourhood clinic, where they immobilised my ankle and recommended at least four weeks of rest, Collins took me to my house. Following the doctor's orders, he sets me on the sofa and places a throw pillow under my ankle.

"You also need ice," he thinks out loud.

Since we left the gymnastics studio, he has taken care of me with a single-minded focus in a way no one has ever done before. It both fills my chest with warmth and overwhelms me.

"Where can I find ice?"

"In the freezer."

He gives me a puzzled look, and I chuckle. Collins is like a fish out of water, and there is something adorable in seeing such a strong and naturally dominant man out of his element *for me*.

"That tall and cold white box in the kitchen. On the top part, you can get a bag of frozen veggies. That will do." I point to the freezer.

He nods, and after a few minutes, he is back with three bags of frozen veggies. He cocoons my ankle with them before I can protest his over-the-top antics.

"Do you need a drink, or perhaps something to eat?" he asks, without coming too close to me.

I am relieved he is giving me space. If he were closer, I might forget my reservations and sprained ankle to act on this desire and jump him. Jesus! I am going crazy.

"Are you hungry?" he asks again, attracting my blushing attention.

At the mention of it, my stomach gets vocal about its needs, growling.

"I will cook something." I am about to collect my crutches to stand up when he rushes closer to me.

"No, little human. You will keep those pretty legs up for me and let me take care of you."

I am at a loss for words, eyes travelling between him and my legs as desire drenches my panties. Why does he affect me so much?

"I-I…" I stutter, so unused to having someone doing things for me that it feels a little uncomfortable. "I can do it. You see, I've always done those things, even when I was sick or had a dance injury." I didn't have another option. Even though I don't live on my own, I was always left to fend for myself.

He furrows his brows and crosses his arms in front of his hunky chest, making his muscles bulge. I swallow hard, as more moisture gathers down there, ruining my underwear.

"You are not alone. I will feed you and take care of you."

"How about when you leave?"

He will leave in a few hours anyway and I will resume my routine of doing things by myself, injured or not. It's not the first time I hurt my ankle or got a lousy dancing wound, and it never prevented me from taking care of myself. It won't be different now.

39

"I cannot leave you hurt on your own. The human healer said that you must rest, apply ice and elevate your leg. That is precisely what you will do, while I take care of you."

My eyes widen, and I gasp in shock. Does it mean that he will stay? That idea fills me with warm fuzzies and sends a cold wave of fright down my spine. I don't want him to leave or... but I am also not emotionally equipped to spend the whole day, let alone days, with Collins. No one has ever stayed for me before. And the fact that he is the person—or merperson—I want the most only makes it that much harder.

With a sigh, I look away from him. I didn't know what he meant by courting, but I surely didn't think he meant moving in with me. I would rather take things as slowly as possible. I grew up witnessing what bad relationships did to my mum, and that's why I've never been in a relationship. Even going on a second date with a guy Olivia set me up with drove me anxious, so moving in with a merman has all my inner alarms flaring up into panic.

Noticing my distress, he kneels next to me and takes my hand in his. His gaze is soft and so is his voice. "You have nothing to worry about, Samantha. In what concerns courtship, we can go as fast or as slow as you feel comfortable with. I will not pressure or coax you, yet I will treat you like the precious beloved you are and take good care of you."

Precious. Beloved. Take care—the words swim in my mind with a tidal force, almost submerging me.

You can do it, Samantha. Being looked after won't hurt, except when he leaves. Everyone leaves; that's a fact of life. And sometimes, those present in your life aren't really there. That's why it has always been only me and my imaginary song.

"Okay," I murmur, half hesitating.

"Now, tell me what you need."

"A shower first. Can you... help me put one of the low kitchen stools in the shower stall?"

How I want to clean the wet mess down there. I shouldn't be nervous about it, right? He can't notice how I am dripping for him. No, it's impossible, but everything about him—about us—is magically impossible.

He nods and does what I ask, also taking me all the way to the shower stall. After I shower and get dressed, Collins helps me to the living room. Once I am settled, I look at my phone, and seeing no new messages, I flip over to check my bank app. I sigh in frustration, looking at the most recent transaction. A reminder that I've spent the money I didn't have to spare at the clinic. I will have to delay my plans to take the reins of my life and move to the dorm.

Collins curses under his breath and grumbles something about damned electric eels, attracting my attention. He struggles in the kitchen, looking at the pans and ingredients like they are alien objects.

"Collins, I appreciate your effort, but that doesn't seem like a good idea. You will either take a long time to make something or end up feeding us plastic with dishwashing liquid." The chances of him burning down the house are also very high.

"You should rest." He exhales.

"I am fine. I like cooking, and you can carry me to the kitchen stool." I try to come to a compromise, even though having him carrying me everywhere in the house is still too much for me.

Once I settle on the stool, Collins hands me all the ingredients and tools I need and watches me make pasta with intent attention. I don't love cooking, but I also don't hate it. It's about making what I need, so I've just learned the basics by doing it. Though, seeing how fascinated he is watching me makes me wish I were better at it.

"What happened to your first beloved?" My eyes go wide, and my hand flies to my lips, slapping them.

Where did that come from?!

I regret the words as soon as they leave my mouth. I used to have a filter. What is happening to me? I should be more sensitive. That subject is none of my business, except something in me needs to know.

Jesus! I didn't hit my head when I fell, so why am I so out of my mind?

"I am so sorry. You don't have to tell me if it's hard for you." Hesitance laces in my voice.

Collins gazes into my eyes. His glossy and darkened eyes reflect the storm brewing within. A heavy Moment passes as he collects whatever thoughts he needs to recount what may very well be a painful memory. When he appears settled, his smile is weak.

"She was a witch, an air elemental and seer. A widow who mothered a young child. We were not able to separate when we discovered the other, and she came to my home in the Queendom of Tal Lashar. She intended to spend only days, then return to the surface to retrieve her child. An unexpected pregnancy foiled her plan. She started feeling sick and indisposed, and we discovered carrying our surprise weakened her. Returning to the surface in such a condition would put hers and the baby's lives in jeopardy." Collins pauses, taking a deep inhale as reliving the painful memories brought a shadow to his face, glooming his bright eyes.

He looks transfigured—-not as if he had seen a ghost, but as if he were the ghost of a man.

I watch with a stuttering heart as his focus turns to the window. I remain silent, not knowing what to say. Finally, breathing a heavy sigh, he returns his focus to me.

"Carrying and delivering a merbaby over the water is dangerous. When her health improved, she was far along in her pregnancy but determined to reunite with her older child. She left the queendom and never returned to me. Death claimed her first, and my daughter... I felt when our baby was born—" He releases a long exhale, his eyes moisten with unshed tears and pain evident in his face.

His song drops to a melancholic note that tugs at my heart. I gulp hard, grief forming a cold ball in my stomach as if I shared his pain. I do share it on some level and I ache for him and his tragic past.

42

"Your daughter—" I choke out the words but struggle to catch my breath.

"My dearest Samantha, do not cry. She lives." He caresses my face, gently wiping my tears.

His daughter might be alright, but his beloved died. For some reason, I understand that it's tenfold worse than losing a spouse. Although the connection between us is new, delicate and feels as easily breakable as a piece of crystal, I have a clue of how strong the bond between soulmates can be—*music uniting two souls.* Nothing can reach deeper than that.

Jesus! None of this makes any sense. It's all so abrupt and absurd.

"I am so very sorry." I swallow back my tears, my gaze fleeting his.

I shouldn't have asked and made him relieve such a nightmare.

"Thank you, but it's not necessary. Wondering is as natural as swimming."

I nod and face him again before my eyes roam to the pasta. "The food is almost ready."

He helps me to put the pasta in two bowls, and soon the awkwardness is forgotten. The sadness in his eyes gives place to curiosity as he studies the simple dish.

He tries a forkful, moaning in approval. The sound is so sexy and deeply masculine that I might have another situation with my underwear. The expression on his face shows how he is enjoying every bit of food, which fills me with joy.

"This is far better than crustacean soup. Thank you, Samantha. You are remarkable."

I chuckle at the compliment. "You need to try real good food. Maybe we can order Chinese tomorrow."

"Chinese? Humans from China, the land bathed by the North Pacific Sea?" His eyes widen in shock.

"No! No! Humans don't eat other humans, there are a few—No, we won't eat people or fish for that matter."

43

"That comes as a relief." He laughs. The sound adds a pantie-melting note to the beautiful song cascading from him.

"Why is the song in my mind louder and more vibrant when I'm near you?" I ask, hoping he doesn't think I am crazy and having musical hallucinations.

"Once one meets their beloved, they can listen to the song of their soul. A multitude of factors, including geographic proximity, amplify the song to a louder tune. I've located you by following your song. It led me straight to the studio. I should have knocked and avoided both the startle and the accident." He let out a heavy breath.

"So, since you met me, you can listen to my song?" I ask, my mind swirling with confusion.

"Yes."

"Why could I listen to your song before I've met you? I don't understand."

"What?" Collins tilts his head back, brows furrowing in surprise. "That's unheard of. For how long have you listened to my soul-song?"

I pinch the inner part of my cheek with my teeth. "I don't know. Since I can remember."

So even within all the oddity of magic, what I feel is not normal. Collins turns to face me, taking my hand in his.

"Gods! That's rather special, Samantha—impossible, but I've come across what was not supposed to occur enough times to…" he pauses, his expression tensing.

"What?"

"To accept that certain things are beyond our understanding, which is not easy to deal with."

"Can't those unpredictable things be good as well?" I ask.

"I am beginning to believe so." He gives me a smile as his song soars, taking my heart in its swell and reaching higher notes.

How can I be angry at him any longer? His rejection still stings even more than my ankle, but he and his song wrap me in a cocoon

44

of peace. Plus, I've never been someone to hold grudges, and doing that with him feels even harder.

Which doesn't mean I will run to his arms. I will control myself, although my body is begging for his touch and my newly changed panties are already drenched. Everything is so natural between us. Collins might be magical, a merman for God's sake, but he feels more familiar than my family ever did. He feels like home.

"Does every creature have a song to their soul, but we—at least we humans—are unable to listen to them?" I ask.

"No, only merfolk. Our souls are a song, and in the rare cases our beloveds aren't merfolk, we can listen to music exuding from their souls."

"How is my song?" I would love to listen to it myself.

His hand roams down my arm, cupping my chin as she leans closer. "Your song is gorgeous, soft, sweet and from time to time it has a breathless crescendo that coaxes me to touch it and make you sing louder. I want to touch your soul, caress it in the strings of a harp as it vibrates for our ears only." Passion and an ounce of possessiveness charge his voice.

My heart thrums as I slant towards him, just as breathless as he described. Collins captures me in his arms, placing me on his lap, and my legs wrap around him. His lips skim over mine and the almost touch is agonising. I skate closer, feeling his hardness against my core. Oh my God! I will melt into a goo.

CHAPTER 6
Samantha

With his hands cradling my face, he brushes his lips against mine. In a moan, I part my lips for him and he accepts the invitation, his tongue sliding into my mouth to caress mine. His kiss is gentle until I moan into his mouth. It flips a switch inside him, and angling my head to deepen the kiss, he claims my mouth—nibbling, licking and sucking at my lips and tongue. He only parts the kiss when I am a trembling heap of desire, unable to breathe or do anything other than accept his claim and take everything he gives me.

Collins scoops me up in his arms, scooting to my room. With delicacy, he lays me on the bed, hovering with me.

"I wanted to court…" his laboured breath cuts his words short. His intense look flicks between my eyes and lips as he continues, "woo you first." He groans as he licks his lips.

Is there a better way to woo me than making me shiver with need?

"You are a very naughty little human." He grins, running his thumb across my lips.

My breath hitches and I jump. Oh my God! Did I say that out loud?

"Very well, my beautiful beloved. If that's the way you want to be courted, I won't deny your request."

After placing a pillow under my injured ankle, he returns to his position to kiss me again. His teeth graze against my lips, coaxing me to open for his hungry kiss as his hand glides down my side. He pulls up my shirt to caress my stomach and trace the hem of my skirt with dextrous fingers.

"Should I stop?" he asks against my lips, his warm breath rising goosebumps across my skin and sending a delicious shiver down my back.

"No. Don't stop," I moan the words, drawing a bright smile from him.

His smile is striking, and I love how his music now vibrates with a joyful tone. It has always had such a melancholic note to it, and now knowing that it reflects his soul, I can't help but hurt for him.

He pauses, eyes trained on mine as he strokes my cheek with the back of his hand. "Are you alright, little human?"

"Yes. I only need more kisses."

His expression lights up at my words and he doesn't hesitate, taking my lips before he leaves a trail of nibbling kisses down my neck. He removes my tank top to expose me to his caresses, and his slightly stubbled jaw grazes at the swell of my breasts before his lips reach there.

I moan and arch my back towards him, eager for more. My nipples ache for his touch, pebbling against my sports bra. I've never been touched there before, not even in my first and only frustrated one-night stand.

"You sing so beautifully, little one. I cannot wait to hear how you moan and mew when I take as many orgasms out of you as you can give me." His voice is an octave lower, and so is his song. His words and tone are so heady that a thick cloud of arousal descends over my brain, fogging my thoughts.

I want. I need. Please.

"Please."

With two fingers hooked on the edge, I try to pull my bra off. Collins helps me and as soon as my breasts are uncovered, he licks circles on one of them before swirling his tongue around my nipple and sucking it as his other hand tugs and twists the other one.

"Oh my God!" I cry out.

He stops, squeezing a breast in the best pain-pleasurable way. "No Gods. I am the only one you will call for when I am claiming you, understand?"

"Yes." My merman God!

I nod as I push my breast into his hand, yearning for him to squeeze it harder. His branding touch is so perfect that I feel as if I've missed it for my whole life.

"Good girl," he praises.

The words work like magic, sending a gush of arousal between my thighs.

Collins licks and nibbles at my other nub, a hand sailing under my skirt to cup my sex. He hisses, cursing under his breath. "You are so wet for me, my good girl."

Yes! I am melting for him. We are moving too fast, but it's too good and I can't bring myself to stop it, although I should.

His gaze locks with mine as he lashes his tongue at my pebble. The intensity and desire burning in his eyes is enough to send a pulse of electricity down to my clit.

I moan louder, winding my fingers in his dark locks. He flashes me a wicked grin before embedding his teeth on my delicate skin, nibbling harder. I scream and squirm under him and we both know it's not out of pain.

How does he know everything I like when I don't know it myself?

He soothes his bite with a long lick, blows air on my wet skin, and then presses a reverent kiss on it. He kisses down my stomach while pulling my skirt up until it's bundled around my waist. When his mouth reaches the waistband of my skirt, he stops.

"Spread your legs open for me, but mind your ankle, little one."

I do as he says, and I am rewarded with his finger trailing along my folds over my blue cotton panties. Now for the first time, I wish I owned sexy lingerie like my sister does. Collins doesn't seem to care as his lips skim down my mound and he kisses my clothed sex.

I need these undies out of the way, now.

As if he can read my thoughts, he rips the waistband off in such a way not to bite at my skin.

I gasp, eyes widening, and Collins flashes me a grin. "I am mindful of your injured leg, and I won't slide those down and risk bruising it."

He pockets my panties and proceeds to run his tongue along my folds. I freeze, remembering what my date once told me about oral sex. *Guys don't like it 'cause' it's gross.*

My hands cover my lower lips, and Collins lifts his head to face me.

"You don't have to do it. I know that guys don't like to do this," I mumble, flushing.

He kisses the back of my hands and flashes me a hungry grin. "You can't imagine how desperately I want to eat you, lap and drink your cum after I make you come as many times as your body can take it. Now be a good girl and let me worship this pretty pussy."

I gape at his words but nod, wanting nothing more than to be his good girl and let him lick me. He kisses my hands again and removes them out of his way, tonguing me from my opening to my clit.

When the mental fog dissolves a little, I catch myself grinding on his face. My cheeks flush with embarrassment. God, I am shameless! With a groan, he licks harder and clenches his teeth on my clit. I leap from the bed, throwing my head back and moaning like a cat in heat.

"Oh my... Collins!" Trembling, I cry out.

His fingers dig into my hips, pinning me in place while he licks my sensitive spot, the spare hand teasing my folds, circling my entrance.

"Please, don't. Inside, please—"

49

"Aren't you an impatient little human? Eager to have your sweet cunt eaten and wrecked? We will get there, baby. Now let me savour you, take my time playing with this pussy." His voice is a raspy caress to my senses, only flaring up my need.

Can anticipation drive me to an orgasm? It does feel like it.

He sucks at my clit as he pushes a finger into me, and my body undulates. On their own accord, my legs wrap around his shoulders. I ignore the slight burn on my ankle, too intoxicated by his skilled mouth to care about anything else.

Collins stops, placing my leg on the pillow and narrowing his eyes at me. "Behave, baby!"

He smacks my inner thigh. After I sing in delight at the pleasurable sting, he grins and does the same with the other leg.

"You are a kinky little human."

Maybe I am a little kinky; everything feels so perfect with him, that I can't say if I have a tiny spanking kink or a huge Collins kink. I only know that his mouth is magical.

He dives in again, wiping off my thoughts with the swirl of his tongue, licking every inch of my folds but my throbbing clit. To my relief, he thrusts a finger into me again and I clench around it. I feel emptier than ever. I need more. Lapping at my clit, he slides another finger inside. I whimper at the stretch but gyrate my hips, eager for more friction and needing more of him.

His fingers swirl inside me until my pussy convulses, the pleasure building up quickly. My body tenses and a knot forms in my stomach. Collins licks me faster, sucking at my clit as his fingers take me harder, exploring spots I've never reached and awakening new and incredible sensations.

When he nibbles at my clit, I come undone, yelping and writhing as a crushing wave of pleasure floods my senses into sweet numbness.

"Collins, please." I don't know what I am asking for. I only know I'm burning for him. He plunges a third finger inside and I scream, the surprise and the stretch too much.

Collins kisses my clit once, then stops and crawls up until his lips are hovering over mine.

He cradles my face as if I were the most precious thing in the world, and his lust-blazing eyes zero in on mine. "I have never been with a human. However, I need to ask. Have you been with a man before?"

He surely can recognize I am a virgin by the situation down there. I can hardly take three fingers.

I shake my head, a little ashamed. Will he think I am a moron? "No, I've done other things, but not that."

Blood rushes up my face, and it heats with embarrassment. Olivia tried to hook me up with a friend of her boyfriend, but it didn't work out. He was tipsy at first, and after a few sloppy kisses, he took me to his dorm room, where I touched him and he clumsily touched me. It was uncomfortable and felt wrong.

After telling me how gross it is for a guy to eat out, he ended up falling asleep before we could take it further. And I can't say I'm not grateful that the booze made him snooze like Olie says. I want my first time to be with my... beloved, even if he thinks I am a silly virgin.

Collins takes my hand in his and covers it with reverent kisses before kissing my lips. I squirm as he cups my pussy, but he pins me in place with his intent gaze, so full of passion and tenderness.

"We can take it slower. I will court you first, learn everything about you and pleasure this perfect pussy before I make love to you."

"That is a good idea." Taking it slower is the right thing to do, even though if he hadn't stopped it, I would be carried away by the heady moment and spent the night with him.

Now in this human form, with legs and everything, he must have a dick, right? And there is the hardness I felt when I wrapped my legs around him in the kitchen.

Collins resumes flickering my clit and my thoughts dissolve into a heated fog once again. He works my pleasure-bundle fast, while easing a finger into me, gentler than before. My stomach coils and I cry out as I climax around his fingers.

"How about you?" I ask in a sleepy voice. He hasn't gotten off yet, only focused on me.

"My sweet Samantha, you do not have to worry about me. Tonight, I only want to court you in the way you chose." He flashes me a cocky smile.

Cocky. Hmmm. I must be out of my mind because I pop the question out loud, "Is that because you don't have a co-cock?"

He furrows his brows for a moment, his jaw thickening. I slap my big mouth, afraid I've offended him, when he bursts out in a drool-worthy laugh, taking my hand to cup his package with it. Surprised at the volume, I take a gasping breath. He is huge, and he is hard, so hard!

"I have lots of cock for you, little human. I will fill you to the brim   and   ruin   your   pussy."

CHAPTER 7
Collins

A sweet song blooms in my mind, resembling the notes of the finest of the harps, raising an unfamiliar urge to reach the surface. Without questioning my instincts, I cross the gate of the Northern Atlantic Sea to rise at the grey waters skirting a seemingly empty beach.

The gentle song ripples, swelling into a tantalising note when my gaze finds her. The most astonishing woman in a blue dress dips her feet into the icy-cold water, ignoring the biting winter wind that whips her skirt around her legs.

Her fingers flutter with ethereal delicacy, hauling a stream of water and making it dance to a rhythm strikingly similar to my heart's thud. Is she a water elemental witch, gifted with the ability to bend the water to her will? As a leaf and a few pebbles join the water swirl in a mesmerising dance, not even the most talented starfish would be able to mimic, I realise I am wrong. She is an air elemental, wielding the winds to carry and coil objects.

Nothing short of hypnotised by her graceful enchantment, and the unmistakable song exuding from her soul, I swim closer to the shore.

She lifts her head, eyes searching the waters until she meets my gaze. My heart stops for a moment and her soul-song consumes me, invading every inch of my being. Her bright green gaze confirms what my soul already knew. She is mine. My soulmate, my beloved, my destiny. And even if she weren't I would choose her, seize her away and give her so much pleasure and love that she wouldn't have any other choice but stay with me, become mine.

Without breaking the delicate string of magic stretching between our locked gazes, she gasps. For a moment, I fear she might turn and flee. I'm aware that the witches in her coven are not fond of my kind. I will prove to her that the feud between our species is a misunderstanding, and I want nothing else than to flood her with music, ecstasy and passion.

Petrified, I stare in disbelief as she runs towards me. Then as though pulled by a force tenfold stronger than gravity, I bolt closer to her.

She stops a few inches in front of me, trembling in the frigid waters.

"Mine!" I claim, capturing her in my arms and lessening her quivering. I need to feel her, touch her, be inside of her.

Putting enough distance between us to cradle her alluring face between my hands, I look into her eyes as my thumb trails along her bow-shaped lips.

"I am Collins, my beautiful beloved."

A heavenly smile forms on her lips, and she covers my hands with her cold, dainty ones. "Sadb."

"Sadb," I repeat, enthralled. Finding one's beloved is so precious and rare. Among my eight siblings, only one has been gifted such a blessing.

I press my forehead against hers, intoxicated by her presence.

"I still can't believe it, or think, only feel it." She motions to our chests, and I know she is talking about this tides-changing connection, the bond singing between us.

Her hand slides down my tail, and I quiver. How can such a casual touch be that arousing?

A primal need transcending desire floods my chest and I trail my tongue along her lips. She parts them for me, granting me access as she presses her body against mine. Her sweet and heady taste explodes on my tongue, coaxing me to kiss her harder, to explore her mouth and ravish her with long licks and nibbles. Sadb is edible and I have every intention to lick every inch of her body, worshipping her completely.

As I tighten my hold on her, trailing a line of licking kisses down her jaw, Sadb's soul-song rises into an enrapturing crescendo, moan-like notes permeating it.

Damnation! If I don't control my impulses, I will end up taking her here and now. Yet my beloved deserves better, to be properly courted and thoroughly loved.

"I want to learn everything about you, possess your body and conquer your heart, my beloved." I cannot wait to both devour and love my beautiful witch.

I wake up with a jolt, sitting up and scrubbing my hands over my face. I should not think about anyone other than Samantha. Yet, after this dream, I am confronted with the feeling that I am betraying them both. Samantha by dreaming and thinking about my former beloved. Sadb's memory and song by being with Samantha and letting her melody wrap around me.

Samantha deserves my undivided attention and my complete devotion to our courtship. Yet, this change of tides and songs was so fast that I am still lost in a maelstrom, torn between my past and my present.

I release an exhale, adjusting my body on the diminutive sofa. My head stings and I have a painful erection after tasting her sweet core, which hasn't softened at all since I left Samantha in her room so she could sleep. After pleasuring my little human a couple times more, I decided to move to the living room under the excuse that I didn't want to risk injuring her delicate ankle.

However, the main reason is my inability to stop myself from devouring her if I were to sleep with her in my arms. Her taste, smell and the breathless notes in her song were driving me insane, to the brink of stealing her away to deep waters and possessing her. Yet, I am not a barbarian and I will always put my beloved first. I will give her what she needs, and what she asks for—to slow down. Regardless of how painfully hard it is, I will give her the time and space she needs.

As the minutes pass, my headache soars and I clench my jaw, grinding my molars in agony. It must be one of the side effects the nymph mentioned. Yet, the pain is bearable enough, and I cannot leave Samantha now that we are making progress. Besides, she is injured and so delicate, I will not leave my precious human alone and risk losing her. Humans are fragile, especially one as petite as she.

I smile as Samantha's fluid movements in the studio replay in my mind. She is independent, graceful, and full of life, flying around in her silk as if she can bend the air to her will.

After a creaking sound of the door opening brings me back from my reverie, Samantha arrives in the living room supporting herself on two crutches.

I frown at her. "Little one, you shouldn't—"

"This isn't my first crutch rodeo, and I will be fine." Moving faster than I expected, she dashes onto the sofa and scoots next to me, placing her head on my shoulder.

"I couldn't sleep. I know I said I wanted to take things slower, but I can't." Turning to look at me, she whispers, "I want you."

My fingers swirl in her pale-blond locks as I cup her pretty face, "Are you sure?"

With a stuttering breath, she bites her lower lip. "Collins, I am throbbing for you. I feel that if you don't touch me, I will burn up."

I cannot resist my beloved. Not only because I have not been with a woman since Sadb died, over twenty years ago, but because

56

beyond being aroused like a kraken in rut, Samantha makes me feel alive.

Her words demolish the walls of my self-restraint, and I gather her up in my arms, rushing to her small bed.

Tomorrow I shall start courting her properly, or as well as I can over-the-sea. Now, I have to be inside her.

"You are the most beautiful melody," I murmur against her lips, eliciting a smile from her and collecting it between my lips in a gentle kiss as I lower her onto her bed. The pearl in my collarbone aches with a need that surpasses physical gratification.

I move one hand from under her and part her legs, caressing her inner thigh with featherlike strokes. I have never liked legs for they are ungraceful sticks, yet Samantha makes them look alluring and sensual. She has the most beautiful pair I've seen since… glancing at her face, watching her chew on her lower lip and how her foam-white skin blushes at my touch, I bring myself to change my train of thought to focus on *her* only.

I reach under her shorts to find that she is not wearing knickers. My naughty girl is indeed eager. Giving her what she wants, I slide my fingers along her slit. My thumb rubs her clit as two fingers slowly enter her.

Samantha moans into our kiss, pulling her top up with my help and proceeding to hook her fingers under the hem of my shirt.

"I will show you how much cock I have for you, little one." I punctuate my words with frantic thrusts of my fingers, drawing soft cries from her.

"Yes, please." Her hand drifts down, cupping my crotch and she gasps once I thrust it onto her palm.

With a grin, I remove my clothes, letting my cock spring free. I hustle a sharp exhale as I glance down. The nymph's concoction did not only give me legs but what I assume to be a human-like shaft— shorter and without the sensitive ridges.

"The potion turned it smaller than usual."

"What?" She gulps hard, eyes shifting between my cock and my face as her fumbling fingers brush against my tip. Her touch flares sparks across my skin, causing my balls to tug and I hiss in pleasure. I will have time to answer her question later, now I need her cunt.

My lips wander down her neck as I return my hand to its rightful place, scissoring my fingers inside her as she yelps before clenching around my digits. So delightfully tight.

With our foreheads pressed together, I align my tip with her drenched entrance and halt, lifting my head to look at her eyes.

It might be plenty, and difficult for a human to understand but we cannot go further until I explain to her that once I am buried deep inside her perfect pussy, there is no turning back in my claim and desire. I will not lose another beloved.

"Samantha, perhaps we should indeed wait." I pause and she narrows her eyes, tilting her head in confusion. "What is about to happen between us is no causal shag, but a bond, a claim. Once I take you as my own, your song will stretch across my soul. The moment we connect, I have no intentions of letting you go. You will be mine, and no force in the sea or lands will change my mind or break this bond."

CHAPTER 8
Samantha

"I don't want something casual. I want you. Don't you dare change your mind. I won't change mine." I don't know where the words come from, but they are true. A day with Collins and I am more sure about him than anything else in my life.

A spell of desire is enveloping me with its tendrils, and I can't and don't want to resist it. My body is aching in a deliciously painful way, screaming for Collins to make me hurt so good.

My slightly trembling fingers caress his shaft as I grind closer to him, brushing my core against the tip of his member. Jolts of electricity scatter through my body at the contact.

He cradles my face, kissing my lips as he inches into me. He is too big, and as much as I want him with every fibre of my being, it's hurting. I yelp into his mouth, but he soothes me with both a reassuring note of his song and gentle kisses. Soon the sting becomes pleasurable as he takes me with slow and shallow thrusts. His thumb circles my clit, adding to the building wave with ecstasy.

I've never known true desire before meeting him. Everything used to be an echo, a dream of what was supposed to be, now he is making it come true. And I want more.

"More," I mumble against his lips, gyrating my hips. He grins, showering my lips, cheeks and chin with sweet kisses before bottoming out into me.

A word builds inside me, vibrating my body as if it were the string of a guitar, but all that leaves my lips is a throaty moan.

Everything is happening so fast, from giving him a chance to have him buried deep inside me. I will worry about it later, for now I just want to feel. It might not be the logical thing to do, but nothing makes more sense than *this*. It feels so *right*, that it eclipses my whole life and makes everything else feel kind of wrong, not enough.

He is the song that lulled and followed me my whole life. Now that he is here, I just want to sing along, use his dick as my microphone as he strums my pussy—and between moans, groans and heartbeats we can compose our own music.

I am not sure about my future or even where I want to be, but I have no doubts about Collins. Nor can I wait. I want to be his good girl and let him do all the wicked things to me.

So, I mewl, "Harder, please. Give me more."

He pumps harder, sliding a hand between us to pinch at my nipple.

Of their own accord, my hands skim down his muscular back, pulling him closer. With each thrust, my heart bursts with longing as if I have missed him and being in his arms even before experiencing it.

His arms are my home, and I won't let go of him as much as he won't of me. I bounce my hips, dancing with him, wanting and taking more.

"Aren't you hungry, little one?"

"I am starving for you and for your cock." Holy damn! I've never been so blunt in my life, but I am ravenous for him, wanting to take everything.

He chuckles, dipping his fingers in my hips to keep me in place as he thrusts hard into me.

"Mine!" he claims, invading my parted lips with his tongue in an all-consuming kiss.

Angling his hips, he reaches a spot that has me crying out and squirming, the pleasure too much for me to deal with.

"I can't," I cry out as he chastises me with another delicious pound.

He stops thrusting and studies my face as his turbo thumb works my clit, strangling pleasure out of the little pebble. "Are you alright? Is it hurting?"

"No… it's too good, too much."

Collins laughs, "You can and will take all the pleasure I will give you, little one. Do you trust me?"

I nod, nails pressing against his back. Collins' eyes fix on mine as he speeds his pace, fucking me fast and deep.

Lightning crosses my body as his song swells into a crescendo, flooding me with pleasure so strong that my eyes clench shut.

"Eyes on me as I make you come, baby," he coaxes, holding my hand. I part my eyelids, and my gaze gets lost in his blue-purple eyes, burning with lust and thrill. "Be a good girl and come for me, now."

A scorching ripple of pleasure so strong that it borders pain storms through me, as if my body was waiting for his command to finally relax and break free from any constraints.

I can't breathe. I can't think. There is only music, his touch and his cock possessing me, filling depths of me I didn't even know existed.

"Collins," I cry out as my core convulses around him, clamping him hard.

"Marvellous, baby. You did so well." Even after the deepest pleasure I've ever felt transports me to another world, I notice the strain in his voice.

He kisses my lips before fisting my hair to angle me, giving his mouth access to my neck. As his thrusts go uneven, he sucks at my skin. A few more shoves of his hips matched by my gyrating motions and he's quivering.

"Mine," he grunts.

Once he spurts his seed into me, his song soars in my soul—the sound of the gentle waves, rising into a harp crescendo and a breathless explosion that sounds like a piano and a violin making love. The milliseconds of silence between the notes are somehow as beautiful as the symphony. The melancholic note that was always there is gone, giving space to a vibrant finale.

"Samantha," he calls.

"Yours," I mumble the word that have been building in my chest since our bodies united.

"And I am yours." He kisses the back of my hands.

With a gentle hand on my injured leg to support my ankle, he flips us around. My arms lace his neck and I snuggle my face against his solid chest, yawning.

His member jerks inside me, and I gasp. Does he want to do it again? I flush at the thought. My blood is aflame with desire and my inner walls clamp around him, revealing that I am a little too sore for that.

I lift my head to level my gaze with his. "Do you… I don't think I can take more now."

"I won't move. I just can't bring myself to leave your precious tight warmth yet, if this is fine for you."

"Don't move," I murmur, loving the feel of his half-mast inside me. So full and perfect. As long as my horny sex doesn't clench, it won't hurt. Yet I know *she* can't make any promises. My entire body and soul are enthralled by him.

He peppers kisses on the top of my head, hands trailing down my spine and sending a rush of goosebumps across my entire body.

"I wish we could sleep like this, but this bed is too small and I might end up crushing your leg." His eyes zero in on my ankle. "Is there a larger bed?"

"My mum's, but it would be beyond weird."

"Do humans have rooms or shell-houses for rent?"

I chuckle, and the vibration has Collins groaning as he becomes fully hard inside me.

"You mean hotels? We do, but they are quite expensive." My voice is a breathless song of pleasure.

"Worry not, my sweet beloved. I have human money. Tomorrow we shall have a larger bed, where I can spread you open for me to feast properly."

Should I let him pay for the hotel for me?

I sigh, chewing my lip as my nerves flutter. Seeing how things went bad with my mum and her boyfriends and her relationships were about gifts, and felt like transactions, I never accept anything from anyone. It is hard enough to bring myself to accept little things from Olivia even after being best friends since we were little.

Collins isn't like my mum's boyfriends and this isn't a normal relationship. I've never been in one, but I am pretty sure this deep connection between us is, for lack of a better word, magical. Still, it isn't easy to change my default configuration as I've learned in the few psychology classes, I've opted to attend last semester. I was always interested in how the mind works and these lectures help me quench my curiosity. I sigh, squeezing my eyes closed and trying to *feel him instead of fear.* I focus on his heartbeat and warmth spreads across my stomach, settling in my heart.

I can do that. I don't need to hold on to my sense of independence. I can trust him.

"Yes, we can do that."

"Is your family coming back home?" he asks, and I tell him the basics about their vacations, Mum and Wyatt.

With his cock still inside me, he asks me about myself and I tell him about my dance major, the guitar classes I instruct and my passion for aerial silk. He listens to every word, attentive eyes on me.

"How about your family? Do you have a job?" I yawn against his chest. I am exhausted, but I don't want to stop talking. I want to hear his voice, his words, to learn everything about him.

"I have a daughter with my first beloved, as you know, and eight siblings. My sister, Melise, the one who snatched you to our queendom, is the high queen of Tal Lashar, while our other siblings are guardians like myself. Each one of us is responsible for one of the seven seas. Mine is the North Atlantic Sea. Melise is a very kind mermaid and has the best and purest of intentions, but from time to time her meddling is excessive, although she is often right. I am glad she intervened."

"Me too." His sister sounds like a fantastic woman. Her words about sailors pop in my mind and I have to ask. "Do mermaids and mermen sing to lure people down into the sea?"

"No. Those are sirens, merfolk have other, less harmful talents, at least inherently. When close enough, my kind can feel the tune of anyone's emotions, whether they be merfolk or not. Which is nothing close to a soul song. It would be akin to compare the ring from your shell-phone to a sea of symphonies. Listening to those emotions attentively, one can begin to comprehend the deepest desires of their hearts. My people have used such a gift in a range of ways. Sometimes, when someone's life was bereft of passion, merfolk called them to the depths of the sea."

I listen, fascinated.

"Once those wanting beings experienced desire, incomparable lust and release, their memories were wiped and they were returned to the surface. Yet their bodies and spirit will remember the passionate night, which they might revisit in dreams. Some ill-intended merfolk employ such a gift to harm and slave others. With large conch shells to capture and resonate one's tune, they use people's desire against them, luring them to the sea like sirens do with their maddening singing. This is something Melise and we guardians try to prevent. However, the oceans are large and deep and cruel intentions tend to hide in the abyssal plain."

64

"It should be hard." I draw a shallow breath, and continue, not knowing where the words come from. "Some people seem to have a special aptitude to take something beautiful and pure and pervert it with their selfishness."

Selfish are the worst fishes.

I am too tired, and my mind is going to odd places. Sometimes like now, words and feelings swarm my mind coming from nowhere. It's like I can feel something without it reaching my brain or making any sense. It has been this way with my longing for Collins, the tune in my mind and hum in my body. I am sure this is about the magic fluttering between us.

With a yawn, I bury my face in his chest again and can't resist moving my hips a little, making Collins harden even more.

He groans, trusting once before grabbing my hips to stop my erotic dance. With a feather light finger gilding down my stretched folds, he blows the words just above my ear. "You are too naughty, little one. Decide, do you want to sleep or be devoured? I won't ruin this little pussy, not today. But I can always eat my favourite meal." He cups my folds possessively, his fingers running to my seam, right where our bodies fuse.

I moan, "I-I... I can't take it."

I really wish I could, but I have to spare my poor vagina now, thinking about the future and delirious nights of cock she and I want to ride. When we were little, my sister always wondered why I didn't want to dress like a cowgirl like her. Now it seems like I've found my inner cowgirl, but I only want to ride Collins. And my... beloved is definitely not like the cowboy next door.

"Samantha?" he pulls his hardness from me and I whimper, waking up from my semi-dozing-nonsensical state.

Now that he isn't inside me, a flip switches in my mind. Crap! I have to take one of Kimberly's emergency birth control tomorrow. I can replace it before she is back. What's happening to me? I've never been so impulsive and reckless before. I am losing my mind.

My mind goes mushy once again as Collins kisses my lips. He settles me in the bed, then stands up. To my disbelief, he throws a pillow on the floor and lays next to my bed.

"Collins, isn't that too uncomfortable?"

"No, I'm used to it. Many shell beds are hard, including the one in my private house."

Private house? I mean to ask it but only a yawn leaves my mouth together with an incoherent mumble and my slumber claims me to dreams of music and breath-taking kisses.

CHAPTER 9
Collins

Once we arrive at the hotel, Samantha goes to shower, and as much as I want to follow her, I don't intrude. Since we headed here, she has been contemplative and silent.

This morning, Samantha and I went to her guitar student's house for a lesson. On the way back, she did not allow me to carry her around, and respecting her fierce need to remain independent, I only steady her when she required help. She glowed during the lesson, playing with such talent and passion that I was rendered speechless, unable to take my eyes from my little muse, as if under a hypnotising enchantment.

All of a sudden, my headache wallops with full force again, making my vision tunnel. I stifle a groan of pain, clamping my fists into balls. The potion is taking its toll on me, yet I can't leave her now.

Fetching my shell-phone from my pocket, I message my daughter to ask her about courting rituals for humans. She may be a witch, but she is far more familiar with humans than me. I have to improve my strategy to conquer my little human, for what I am currently doing does not seem to work. Samantha is too distant and seems hesitant, perhaps regretting giving me a chance.

Damnation! The sole thought of having her change her mind sends a trickle of ice into my veins and my anxiety soars, making my chest clench.

My shell-phone vibrates, signalling that my daughter replied, and I open it to read her message.

"Flowers, pralines, a romantic date on the beach. Foot rubs, but not on the first date. Food! Food always works, especially chocolate. That is the way to a woman's heart."

"Thank you, sweetheart."

"I am glad you are dating. I hope she deserves you and your big heart," she replies.

She couldn't be more mistaken, for I am the one who is struggling to deserve Samantha. I huff out a breath, certain that Melise shared her worries about my erratic behaviour—oscillating between apathetic and grumpy, as she puts it—with my daughter. I want to ease their worries, yet nothing is certain with Samantha and I am still concerned myself.

Will she remain guarded and distant due to our first interactions?

Damned abyssal plain! I hope Melise did not tell my daughter about what Samantha is to me, in case it all fails and she rejects our bond.

I won't allow it to happen. I am determined to flood her body with desire and ripple at her heart with care until she is convinced that she is mine.

They sell food downstairs. I will fetch some chocolate for Samantha and search for flowers. As I rush towards the door to head to the lobby, a whimper coming from the bathroom has me halting in my tracks.

"Are you feeling well?" I ask against the door, my hand on the knob and my heart thudding in my chest. The possibility of having my little human in pain fills me with uneasiness.

"N-no," she murmurs, and I don't miss her stuttering breath.

Bursting the door open, I come across a trembling Samantha, shrinking in the bathtub. She is struggling to breathe.

I rush closer to her, and comb the hair away from her face, revealing her blanch cheeks.

"What's happening?" I wrap my hands around her cold shoulders.

"The water," she mumbles with difficulty. "I-the drowning came back to me and I can't breathe. I can't move."

Grabbing her around her ribs, I lift her to me and sit her on my lap so she can feel my body heat. I fetch a towel to cover her pebbling skin.

"You are safe, Samantha. Look at me." Draping my hand around her neck, I swipe my thumb on her discoloured lips, coaxing her to look up. "Follow me. Breathe in, breathe out." Once I see she pulls in a shaky, but deep breath, I continue, "draw slow breaths, and count with me, one, two, three."

After another trembling inhale, she starts, "One." Our fingers intertwine and her gaze rivets on mine as she breathes in again. "Two."

"You are doing so well. Once more, my brave little human," I coax her.

Samantha nods and does as I say. "Three."

We do it a few times until her breath steadies and her cheeks recover their natural rosy colour. I wrap the towel around her and promptly lift us.

Dashing to the bed, I place her under the covers to warm her, but just as I lift off the bed to collect one more towel, Samantha's arms wrap around me.

"Stay, please."

I lie next to Samantha, setting her head on my chest. Gently, I brush her wet hair from her forehead and pull her body closer to me, enveloping her in my embrace.

"I am not going anywhere."

"I've never experienced that before." She sighs.

"Some merfolk that stayed too long on the surface and were unable to breathe experienced the same. It's natural," I try to reassure her, knowing this is not my strongest suit.

"It makes sense, but I hate it and want it to go away soon. I've always loved the water."

I press a kiss on the top of her wet hair. "Try to relax."

As she snuggles into my embrace, I cover her with the duvet, ensuring she is warm and comfortable.

You are safe now, my little human. I won't let anything hurt your mind or body.

From what I've experienced with my people, this kind of trauma didn't fade away in a matter of a tide change but took many moons to heal.

Of course, she is experiencing surface PTSD—or rather water PTSD—after what she has been through. Yet my beloved has been so resilient that the concern wasn't at the top of my mind.

I must help her face her trauma, or at least soothe some of her worry, which also means not bringing up the fact that I should be back underwater soon.

I can wait. What I cannot do is see my beloved in agony.

Samantha doesn't need additional stress. She needs a safe haven, someone to take care of her, for it is evident she grew up bereft of such attention.

"Samantha, are you feeling better?"

She doesn't reply, and listening to how even her breath is, she has fallen asleep.

"I will take care of you, little one."

Kissing the top of her head again, I set out on my mission to find her some food. Following my daughter's advice, I order chocolate from something called room-service. I found a pamphlet about it sitting on the side table next to the human device similar to my shell-phone. Once it arrives, I settle in next to her.

Lying beside her, I revel in the delight of her body next to mine as sleep calls for me to join her.

70

I wake up with a start, my heart thudding as I feel a wet heat pushing into my groin. My temptress moans my name in a whisper while threading her fingers through mine. I remain still, waiting to see what she will do next. Her little tongue skimming along her pink lips sends me teetering over the edge, prompting me to grip her hips and pull her to me as I push forward.

Samantha gasps with a surprised yelp and attempts to roll away from me. Catching her around her middle, I pull her flat against my chest. Mindful of her injured ankle, I roll us so we are upright on the edge of the bed, facing her awaiting surprise.

"Good morning, naughty girl," I smile. She is in trouble for stirring my desire and there is nothing I want more than satiate both of us.

Her face flushes with a sweet blush that has my balls tugging. "Collins, I—"

I silence my beloved with a kiss and only let go when she is breathless.

With my little human safely in my arms, I uncover the food I ordered earlier. Reaching over to sink my finger into what I think is chocolate, I watch her as her brows lift with surprise.

"Where did it come from?" she asks.

"Something called room-service. Now let me court you like humans do."

She giggles. "This is literally so sweet!"

I feed her the first taste in anticipation. My eyes are riveted on her tongue as she licks my fingers, a soft mewl escaping her. The way she laps those lips as she pulls back has my cock thickening with yearning, and I don't want to stop.

I trail a piece of the exotic delicacy along her lips, earning an edible moan from her. My cock stirs further with the need to eat and fuck her again. Soon. If her pussy is still too sore, I will lick it better.

The little temptress licks my fingers, sucking one into her mouth. I push it deeper, revelling in the feeling of her warm tongue against it. Pulling the towel loose, I roam a chocolate-covered finger down her skin, reaching her nipple. Once the melted delicacy is spread on her pebbled point, I suck it clean.

"This is delicious." She moans, arching her trembling body towards my mouth. My pearl pulsates at the soft sound.

I repeat the gentle assault with her other nipple and she grinds herself on my shaft. She is playing with a tidal wave and soon she might find herself submerged under my body, taking my cock to the hilt.

Steading her tantalising movements, I try to give her one more piece of chocolate, but she giggles, pulling my hand away.

"What's your plan, death by chocolate? I love it, but there is only so much I can eat."

I shove the chocolate bar away from her, my eyes wide with terror. "Can humans die this way?" I know they are fragile, but I didn't imagine that I could kill my beloved with sweets.

"No. Only werewolves die that way." She laughs before meeting my concerned expression and pausing. "I was joking, because dogs can't eat chocolate... Wait, do they exist?"

"They do. My sister used to have one in her harem."

Melise always had a large harem brimmed with a vast range of creatures. I am certain she had one or two humans there, decades ago.

"Your sister sounds like an extraordinary woman. I felt that when I met her, but everything I hear makes me like her more."

A wave of jealousy swarms my mind, and I narrow my eyes. "Would you like to have your own harem?"

"If there are many clones of you there, yes." She flushes, coating a finger with melted chocolate and spreading it on my lips before licking them.

"One is enough to fulfil all your needs, I assure you." I grin, flipping her around to lay her on her back. "Now it is my turn to eat."

"But I have to finish the essay for behavioural psychology." Her gaze shifts between me and her laptop on the accent table.

She has already told me that this is the only homework she has on her break and the deadline is approaching. Who am I to stand between her and her education? I hand her the laptop and remove her underwear as she stares at me with rounded eyes. Instead of replying, I settle between her silky legs.

"Collins, what are you doing?" She moans, jerking forward when my finger brushes her folds and my tongue comes in contact with her clit.

Pulling back to admire such a beautiful pussy, I reply, "I am eating, by all means, complete your assignment. We too have universities under the sea, and I know how hard it is to find time to study." My hand dashes to my rock-hard cock and once my meal is laid out perfectly in front of my face, I stroke my shaft in time with my tongue.

Samantha lays her laptop on her propped-up knees and starts typing, while I slide my tongue into her, lapping at her tight cunt. My thumb finds her swollen clit, working on it fast and with a high-pitched moan, she tries to move away.

"I-I," she stutters breathlessly.

Lifting her higher so I have a full view of my dinner, I say. "Give me one orgasm and I will order more food while you finish your work." Relenting, she pushes her laptop to the side, looking at me with hooded eyes.

"Yes, please." My good girl moans, riding my face in time with her own song.

I thrust two fingers into her, rejoicing on how she clamps around them. So wet and ripe to be taken. Soon, I shake my head, focusing on my feast. Lapping her clit with long licks and twisting my digits inside her tightness, I coax a loud orgasm out of her in record time.

True to my word, I order dinner as she works on her paper. After we eat, I have my dessert between her legs again. For an inexplicable reason, tasting her and being inside of her lessens my headache. The bond between beloveds has plenty of nuances my kind is not aware of, for it's so rare.

Lazily spread to cover my body, her fingers wander across my chest. Having her in my embrace eases all my uncertainties. I've never been so insecure, not even when I was a little fish, but the petite human in my arms and the terror of losing my second-chance beloved—my miracle—wrack my convictions.

I tighten my hold on her, wistful that my hold and caresses will suffice. It won't be easy, for we belong to two different worlds and my beloved is too young. Damnation! All humans are far too young. Yet, I am determined to gain her trust and her love. Tomorrow, I shall court her with more than chocolate and my tongue.

Her words bring me back from my contemplation. "I meant to ask you about it yesterday but ended up falling asleep. Is that a tattoo?"

Her fingers wander across the design on my collarbone until it reaches the pearl in the middle. The pearl gleams and pulses, sending jolts of pleasure straight to my cock, eliciting a grunt of sheer delight.

"No, this is the vessel of my soul. The merfolk's essence is harboured in their pearls, and every mer-creature is born with one. The common people have theirs on their wrist, while the pearl of a guardian is set on their collarbones. Melise's is in her forehead, forming a natural tiara."

"It's so beautiful when it shines," she muses.

"It glimmers when I am aroused," I explain.

With a soft gasp, she traces the pearl again and I tremble as a stream of moans leave me.

"It's sensitive." She grins, teasing it further.

"It is, just like the fins in my tail. If you don't want to be pinned to this mattress by my cock, I advise you to stop, little one," I warn, the smidge of humour in my voice shocks me. So long I haven't heard that, either in my voice or my song. Samantha's mere presence is a balm to my soul. She is the life and the music I thought I had lost forever.

Yet that's too much pressure to lay on someone so young and I refuse to do that to her. She is too precious to be crushed by my needs and expectations.

She giggles, attracting my full attention. "I will cash in on this *warning* another day. Now I have a couple of questions."

"Can you feel what's the deepest desire of my heart?" she asks.

When I am with Samantha, her soul song is all-consuming to the extent that I haven't caught her heart's desire yet. Raising her chin, I gaze into her profound green eyes and I am almost struck with thoughts that aren't supposed to surge in my mind. She is *not* similar to Sadb.

I clamp my eyes shut, drawing a sharp exhale and look at Samantha again, seeing her face only—blonde hair instead of dark curls, pink cheeks instead of pale ones.

Longing radiates from her, and an ache lies there so profound within her heart, that I cannot access it and I doubt she can, either.

"It's rather odd, but I cannot feel anything but longing pulsating from your heart."

With anyone else, I would be able to sense more. It is supposed to be easier with the woman whose song soars for my own, yet it is not. Perhaps there is something blocking her or *us*.

Her forehead creases, but she nods. "I do have many longings, so intense that I can't begin to understand them."

She bites her bottom lip, and a blaze of desire vibrates in her gaze. Her hands reach down my body until she finds my cock. With fumbling fingers, she glides along my shaft. The touch is delicate and trembles with uncertainty, yet the light caresses are enough to entice an immediate throbbing erection.

"I want you in my mouth. But I've never done this."

I lift her chin for her to look at me. "I can show you how, little one."

"Teach me, big one." She smiles, and I am unsure if there is a thread of teasing in those large innocent eyes. My only certainty is how much I yearn to thrust deep into her mouth until tears well in her eyes.

Lifting her from my body, I position us so I am standing in front of her as she sits on the edge of the bed, eyes on my cock as she resumes her tentative strokes.

She licks her lips, nervous eyes dancing between my face and my shaft. I take her small hand in mine, guiding it to the base. I pull her hand up and down my length, showing her the pace I enjoy.

"Open your mouth, baby," I instruct, leaning her head until her breath blows on my leaking tip.

As I move her forward, the head of my cock brushes her bottom lip.

"Start at the tip. Take it between those pretty lips."

Samantha doesn't move for a moment, hesitating before sticking out the tip of her tongue to glide it down the head of my shaft. I groan in delight, which emboldens my girl to lick it again. To my surprise, Samantha pulls herself forward, rubbing her tongue from the base to the tip, and laps the pre-cum bead at once. She wraps her small hand around my base, and I encase it with mine to guide her movements. Her warm tongue has my cock jerking with anticipation.

"Now, suck the head in like the good girl you are."

Her lips wrap around my tip and I remove my hand from hers, encouraging her to continue with a look.

"You are doing great, baby. Take more in, suck me like you did my fingers. You are a natural, and these perfect lips were made to suck my cock."

She moans at my filthy words, taking a few more inches in.

"Do you like when I talk to you like you are my perfect little whore, only mine to fuck, and pleasure?" And love.

She hums, sending a delicious vibration down my balls. Holy damned Triton! She is marvellous.

I collect the abandoned chocolate bar on the table and melt its edge between my fingers. As Samantha's mouth slides up to my tip, I coat my length with the melted creamy sweet. She giggles around the head of my cock before taking almost all of me in.

"Clean it like you did with my fingers."

She lifts her head to look into my eyes. Heeding my instructions, she takes a sharp inhale before swallowing a few more inches and stroking her soft tongue against my sensitive skin.

"That's it, little one. Keep going. If you keep doing it as well as you are, I will reward you with my cum." I stroke her hair.

When she hums at my praise, I tighten my grip to tug at her locks. My fingers reach down and wrap around the nape of her neck as I move both my hips and her head to increase our pace.

"Then I'm going to come in your mouth, my dirty little beloved. You're going to swallow every bit of what I give you. Do you understand?"

She gives a tight nod.

"Hands on my balls, feel how heavy they are, loaded for you." I place her hands below my sack.

At first, she cups my balls with hesitance. I release a loud groan when her fondling fingers brush against me, cursing under my breath, which boosts her confidence and her touch grows firmer.

Her velvet-tongue works fast, surely wiping all the chocolate off. That's the best courting threat, a gift that keeps on giving.

To my astonishment, she takes more of my hardened dick, and my tip presses against the barrier of her throat. I hiss a breath, releasing a feral groan. Samantha's eyes fix on mine as she takes my tip down her throat.

"My fucking perfect girl!"

She sucks me harder, gagging for a moment before her muscles relax.

"Is it too much?" I ask.

77

She replies by bobbing her head to pull me to her tight throat.

"My girl is hungry. I will quench your thirst, baby."

She sucks harder, moaning around my shaft.

"Breathe with your nose. Close your throat around me. I will fuck your mouth, but if you want me to stop, squeeze my thigh."

She hums her consent. With a hand on the side of her head, I steady her to thrust harder. My good girl swallows my cock, taking everything I'm giving her. Tears gather at the corner of her eyes and she looks ethereal and sinful with her mouth full of my cock. Absolutely beautiful.

My balls pull close to my body, my back stiffens, and my stomach clenches. I can't hold back any longer.

"I'm about to…"

I try to pull her away, but she moves my hand off her chin. Bobbing her head towards my belly, she swallows down my seed as my orgasm rips through my body. I watch her throat work before my eyes lock with hers. After the last pulse pushes through me, I groan as I pull my spent cock out of her mouth. She coughs, clearing her throat.

"You did perfect." I pant, collecting a thin string of cum from the corner of her mouth and pulling it back past her parted lips.

She swallows it, licking her lips to ensure she got every single drop. The motion floods me with a tide of lust and I can't take my gaze away from that sinful mouth.

"Your mouth is sublime, little one. I didn't expect you to swall—"

"You promised me your cum if I were good, and I'm pretty sure I aced it." Her voice is croaky and her smug grin has me aching to dive into her once again. But I gather her in my arms instead, my fingers rubbing gentle circles on her lower back.

She places a kiss on my chest before reaching my lips.

"I… I've never had so much fun. Thank you for your court gift." My little wanton blushes.

My lips brush on hers. "And I haven't experienced that much joy since... for decades."

I tense, fearing that she caught the meaning behind my words when her expression goes serious for a brief moment, making me regret what I said. But a smile rises on her face, brimming my chest with delight.

"I hope we have many days like this."

Her words mirror my desire. For that's what I want, nights and days of pleasure and joy with her in my arms.

CHAPTER 10
Samantha

I wake up to the desire coiling in my lower stomach, sending heated need through my bloodstream. A soft smile forms on my lips. Waking up in his embrace feels so good. My chest is filled with peace and my panties are a drenched chaos.

My body tingles, still revelling in the pleasure that was last night. Without opening my eyes, I turn around in Collins' arms, pressing our chests together and the contact ramps my need for him. Lost in the memories of last night—the feeling of him coming deep down my throat—I barely register his hand wandering along my arm.

Opening my eyes, I come across his delicious smile.

"Good morning, little one," he murmurs in a sexy morning voice.

He lifts my chin to pepper a soft kiss on my lips and I pull him closer, parting my lips to give him everything. I want nothing but to drown into our kiss.

"I've been waiting for you to wake up. Would you like some breakfast before you leave?"

I am hungry for something else.

"Good morning... I need... you." The words come out in a breathless moan. I am out of my mind and wrapped in a thick wave of desire.

He wraps a hand around my nape, holding me to him as his other hand slowly roams down my body, sliding under my top to caress my nipple. Taking the pebble between his fingers, he tugs at it, sending a wave of yearning straight to my aching clit.

I release a stuttering breath as goosebumps break across my skin.

After rolling and pulling my nipple once more, his hand reaches down to caress my folds. I gasp as he finally dips a finger into me, gathering my arousal to spread it across my clit.

He flicks me with quick circular movements, but as soon as I am on the edge of ecstasy, his movements lose tempo. Oh my God! I can't take it any longer.

"Collins!" I protest.

He crashes his lips against mine in a passionate kiss as his fingers reach down, swirling around my opening.

"Do you want me to wake you up by burying my cock deep inside this pussy from now on?" He blows the words against my lips.

I gasp, but nod. I would like that very much.

His eyes are intent on mine, vibrating with a pantie-melting intensity. "Do you want me to take this pussy whenever I please? Whether you are awake or not?"

The thought of being this close, having him seated deep inside me when I wake up, makes me gush with arousal.

"Yes. Please." I rotate my hips, trying to take his fingers deep and put an end to his torturing teasing.

I need it all, and I need it now. I want this man more than I thought I could possibly want someone.

"Very well. This cunt is mine to pleasure and use at my whim."

81

He thrusts his fingers all the way in, curling them inside me to reach a spot that has me writhing.

"Oh my… Collins!" I cry out, bouncing my hips to fuck myself onto his fingers.

After one more rough thrust, he withdraws and I can almost hear my pussy groaning in protest.

"No, Collins, I need—" Before I conclude my sentence, he rolls us, placing me on top of him. With his firm hands on each side of my hips, he lifts me, positioning me to straddle his face.

The position is so wicked and decadent, and I am completely open for him, my pussy hovering only a few inches above his mouth.

"Ride my face. Take everything you want, little one. Use my tongue to chase all orgasms your eager pussy is begging for."

Holding onto the headboard for support, I take a deep inhale in an attempt to let go of all my inhibitions. After one more look at his purple-blue eyes, hooded with lust, I do as he says, sitting on his face.

Collins slides his tongue into me, taking me with quick thrusts as his nose presses against my clit. I buck onto his face, driving my needy core onto him and all the pleasure I want—I need.

He holds my hip with one hand and the other one roams up my body, cupping my breast and pulling my nipple in a deliciously chastising way. The pang of pain only adds to my pleasure.

I bounce up and down on his mouth to chase my orgasm, forgetting all my worries and the world around us to focus only on him and the pleasure he etches into every cell of my body. His song soars with joy, reaching a beautiful crescendo. He is taking as much pleasure as I am. This knowledge, this connection, is what I need to fall over the edge.

I writhe, crying out his name as an intense orgasm consumes me almost in time with my alarm clock. It's time to wake up and face reality.

I come down the crest of ecstasy as fast as I climbed it. I draw a long exhale. The world and all worries come crashing back on me.

As soon as my breath is even again, I move away from Collins. "I have to shower and change."

I slump into the accent chair and take a deep inhale. I was beyond embarrassed after our first night. Now I'm confused.

It's all too fast. I barely know him, except I do. Sometimes I feel like I know this stranger more than I know myself.

I sigh, almost unable to focus on Noah. My student looks between me and the guitar, a question in his brown eyes.

"I am sorry, Noah. Can you start the intro again?"

He nods, doing as I ask and I spend the rest of the class doing my best to concentrate only on him. Unlike yesterday morning, I insisted on Collins waiting for me in the hotel and took a taxi to Noah's place.

I need some time by myself to think.

I can't make sense of these strong feelings. How can I want and like someone that much after a couple of days? I can't be like my mum, quickly infatuated by a new boyfriend, until everything breaks, and he hurts her.

Collins is different, I repeat to myself, as if it is a chorus. My body and heart understand it, and so does my soul—a humming music box of delight. Yet my mind doesn't catch up.

Being with him, having sex, talking or even doing nothing feels natural. Every moment with him seems to drive me closer to home.

Noah finishes his song, and my mind flips back to the moment. This time I heard everything, and he is as great as ever.

"Soon you will be the one who needs to give me lessons. You are so good, kid!" I ruffle his hair and Noah laughs.

He is thirteen and has been taking lessons with me for the last two years.

Noah stands up to collect his guitar box. "I am happy to see you like this. You seem different." He absently throws the words over his shoulder.

"Different how?"

"You seem happy, like you are glowing. You know, just like I felt after I started playing guitar, like stuff started making sense."

I startle at his words. Noah was always quite in tune, wise for his age, but he is reaching a new level.

"I guess you're right." I smile, taking my crutches in my hands. "See you on Monday."

Noah helps me out by opening the door and I call a taxi to head back *home*—the place Collins is. This time, I will try to *talk*, without ending up with him buried deep inside me or his tongue teasing... Oh my God! Remembering it doesn't help.

Walking into the hotel room, I gasp in astonishment as I take in the swarm of flowers in all colours and shapes and a heap of pralines covering the large bed, desk, chairs, and accent table. There are even a few daisy bouquets on the floor.

"Oh my God!" He really went over the top.

With an arm around my waist to steady me, he asks, "Do you like it? My daughter told me that this is part of the human courting rituals."

It's too much but I smile. "I love it! Thank you!"

No one has gone that out of their way for me before. I've actually never gotten a single flower and this... it's extraordinary!

I swirl around and throw myself into his embrace. Without losing time, he scoops me up into his arms and kisses me. Flinging the objects onto the floor, he clears up the shelf and sits me there, leaning between my thighs. *We can talk like I wanted to later. Now I need him.*

"Are you still sore?" he asks.

"No, just aching for you," I say, forgetting my hesitancy and my shyness—which is almost gone since yesterday's choco-sucking and this morning's before-breakfast feast.

It's like I am possessed by someone else, a very naughty lady obsessed with his… cock, and I love every second of it!

At my words, a bright smile forms on his face and he kisses me, murmuring against my lips, "I will give you everything you want and need, little one."

When I am with other people or alone, my mind always wanders to songs and plans, pretty much anywhere. I have never really been in the moment. But it is different with Collins. He occupies all my thoughts and I feel present as if there is no other place and time I would rather be.

In a matter of seconds, he removes my shirt and bra as I bundle up my loose blue skirt around my waist. He parts my legs, making sure that my ankle is comfortable. With a tug on the seam, he tears my panties and cups my exposed core. His fingers run from my opening to my clit and he licks his lips, eyes intent on me.

"You are so wet for me, my good girl."

Always. Everything about Collins is wet, the sea, my pussy. He is just… I stop my insane line of thought and nod at him, murmuring the words as my cheeks heat with a flake of shyness, "I need you inside me now, not your fingers or tongue, but your… cock."

He laughs, throwing his head back and the carefree sound adds to his song, forming the most delicious chorus. I am salivating from my mouth and sex alike.

"Everything you need, now open this pretty pussy for me."

With a hand on my stomach, he leans me back to the shelf until I am spread open for him. He guides my hands to my lower lips to show me what he means.

85

"Keep your hands there," he commands.

My clit pulses like a second heart at the authority in his voice. I definitely must be possessed by a nympho, but now all I want is to be *possessed by him.* He teases me instead, running his tip over my slit in slow-motion.

I clench my eyes and moan out the words. "Please. I need it."

I might be a good girl, but Collins is wicked, and so is his cock.

"Look at me while I fuck you, baby." He tilts my chin up and my eyes are trained on his as he slides into me and fills me to my limit.

I wince, and he stops moving. "Tell me to stop if it's too much."

It is too much, and he is too *big*, but I don't want him to stop. I need him to hurt me good until pleasure and pain twine into ecstasy.

"More," I cry out instead.

He shoves his hips harder, bottoming out and even the sting of the stretching is delicious. My eyes cross as I gyrate my hips as much as I can, dancing for him. He angles his hips as he pumps into me and my pussy clamps. I am about to come!

No! Damn! We need protection. This realisation strikes me and my muscles tense, all the pleasure replaced by worry. I remember sex-ed classes, taking the emergency pill that close to the last time would make it as effective as a mint. The pill isn't an option.

"Collins, I am not taking any kind of contraceptive." Panic undulates in my voice.

He will freak out and pull out before it's too late.

Instead, he quickens his thrusts and flashes me a grin. "Good. I will put a baby inside of you now. You are mine, Samantha."

"I-I… are you—" I moan and stammer at the same time.

"You shouldn't have any doubts that I will always want you, Samantha—you and all the babies we will make."

He pumps harder, wrapping his fist around my hair to pull me close. A wave of heat floods my body, my lower stomach tingling as my pussy clenches around him. Arching towards him, I cry out in delight. His words are all I need to explode in a strong orgasm.

"This isn't casual, baby. I want you forever." He punctuates each word with a deeper thrust until his movements go uneven.

With a groan that could be mistaken as a growl, he spurts into me. The twitches of his cock have my pussy clenching as if it wants to make true of his words and milk him to the last drop.

His hand brushes against mine on my folds and I gasp when I see that he is pushing the leaking cum back inside.

"You were serious?"

"Absolutely. You are mine." To my disbelief, he is already full-mast and thrusting back into me. "Is that what you want, Samantha? It is your decision."

My body has no doubts, my heart is screaming with joy, but my brain says: *slow down, cowgirl!*

He cups my face, pressing a tender kiss on my forehead. "No pressure, little one. I can still find an effective contraceptive potion for you today."

I nod, postponing the insane decision to future Samantha. I am becoming a reckless nut job, but I've never been so happy, so who cares?! Since I am already wet, I might as well dance in the rain.

Minding my ankle, I wrap my legs around him, pulling him deeper into me. We moan in tandem, lips locking in a feverish kiss.

His words surge back in my mind, and my heart expands in my chest. *I want you forever.* An eternity with him sounds… perfect.

I think I have more feelings for him that I can admit to myself. I am falling in love. Nothing will brace the fall and I might break my butt and my heart instead of my ankle this time. But the fear of falling never prevented me from flying winged by my silks, and it won't start now.

Collins pulls me into another long kiss, and I feel our songs sync, rising to a crescendo. It's the first time I hear my song and I love how it twines with his. They are perfect together.

When he is deep-seated inside me and our gazes meet, the world seems to dissolve into a soul-bending melody. Images flash before my eyes, high cliffs and the grey sea. A brunette mane blows in the wind.

The song swells louder than ever and it is as if I can taste and smell it. It carries his sea-breeze scent and is a salty delight. I blink a few times and Collins' purple-blue eyes are in front of me again, the gleam in them resembles stars. My heart races and a wave of longing ripples through me.

"Mark me," I gasp at my words, not knowing where they came from or what they mean.

Collins' eyes widen but his shock morphs into a bright smile. "I will, my precious pearl, but not like this. Once I take you under the sea, to my–our–home, I will mark you. I will wait for however long it takes until you are ready to come home with me. Then, I will give you my mark, and although I am no king, I will make you my queen."

CHAPTER 11
Collins

I slow my thrusts as I stare at her etched with the same amusement and bewilderment one has gazing at the stars.

She wants me to mark her. Merfolk do not mark their beloveds. There are only two exceptions, which are nothing short of a miracle.

Unbeknownst to that, my little human asked for my mark. So, a third miracle shall take place, uniting our souls at a more profound level that our shared songs could reach.

Cradling her face, I kiss her lips and my thrusts gain tempo. I rub at her clit to take her to the apex of pleasure with me. Samantha releases a soft cry and as our songs soar in unison, we orgasm together.

I press my forehead against hers, revelling in her gasps and the soft sounds of her riding down her ecstasy.

Once she recovers her breath, she starts, "I can't go under the sea with you now. I don't think I can be in the ocean that soon." A note of panic charges her song. I hold her against my chest, attempting to soothe her. "And I... I want to wait at least until my family and best friend are back to talk to them in person before I go. There are also my students, the ballet school and–" Samantha says in one quick breath.

I can't hold back the large smile forming on my face. In response, Samantha gives me a confused look.

"I am thrilled you consider going there."

"Collins, I know it's insane and everything is happening so soon and fast, but I want to give this a chance and it makes sense to go to your home, even if only for some time. I liked it there, it felt ..." Gulping hard, she changes subjects as her gaze darts to the ceiling for an instant. "I don't know what's happening to me. I was out of my mind not to say something about birth control earlier. Sometimes I feel like two people in one. This bond is so strong. The baby talk as a sexy thing is okay, but we can't have a baby now." Her teeth graze at her bottom lip before she murmurs the words, "I'm afraid of forever."

I tighten my hold on her, my fingers drifting down her white-blonde locks.

I hope my reassurances and the constancy of my love and lust will dampen her fear. The fact that she asked for my mark and is willing to travel under the sea with me are great indicators that we are making progress.

I want her and our future together with an intensity and urgency typical of merfolk. Our emotions mirror the immensity of the boundless sea. Which is something humans and other terrestrial creatures would fail to understand. However, I would never pressure her on the matter—neither regarding travelling to Tal Lashar, nor having children.

She draws a long sigh, bringing me back from my contemplation.

Lifting her chin, I reassure her, "You are coping with all the novelty and changes very well. You are remarkable, Samantha."

I am extremely proud of how brave and open-minded she is, something my people didn't often find in humans, in the few encounters between our species that I am aware of.

"I like these changes. They feel *right*."

Although many say an old fish can't handle an abrupt change of tides, I will whole-heartly embrace all changes she elicits, even if she is to redesign the stars and the courses of the currents. I *love* the novelties she is bringing to my life after I'd grown to think there was nothing else for me anymore—no future, no thrill, no love. Samantha brings these three miracles to me.

"How about the contraceptive potion you mentioned? Do you have to return to the oceans to get it?" she asks, attracting my full attention back to her pretty flushed face.

"No. Those potions are normally brewed by witches. I can find the coven in this region and buy it there. Most covens have a small market or shop."

"Do they have witch covens here in Texas? Some cowgirl witches too?" She giggled, amused.

My brows furrow in confusion. "Cowgirls? I know little about cows, except their quadruplet condition."

Samantha laughs. "I will show you what I mean later. How about the covens?"

"I am certain I can find a few covens nearby. There are plenty of covens around the lands and other magical creatures also roam about it. Magic surrounds humans and it always has."

I have to ask my daughter for the address of the nearest coven. She can easily find it on Witch-Net. I am relieved she is not a nosy fish like her aunt and won't question me about it.

"That's incredible! I wish I could meet them. On Halloween, I've always loved to dress like a witch." She smiles, arms lacing around my neck to pull me in for a kiss.

Parting our long and passionate kiss, I create some distance between us. "One day I can take you to a coven, but today I shall hurry so that you have your concoction on time. About coming under the sea with me, take your time. There is no need for haste."

I will have to find another solution for the potion's increasing collateral effects. Departing from Samantha is not an option and I won't pressure her to leave her entire life behind and face the sea when the bathtub is enough to spike her panic.

Once I am crossing the hotel hall to return to the bedroom, my shell-phone rings. I am back from the coven with both herbs to prepare Samantha's contraceptive tea and an elixir to relieve my searing headaches.

As soon as I open the shell-phone, Melise starts, "Collins, I cannot believe the risk you are taking. Bring your tail, alas lack thereof, back under water!"

"Zoe told you about the potion?" I shouldn't have trust in the nymph's discretion, for it seems like everyone in Tal Lashar, she has the harrowing habit of being meddlesome.

"No, she didn't. It was a crab. You know how crabs are, they talk. Crabs are small, easy to hide in any cleft or spot and very prone to gossip, which would make them the perfect spies if they were capable of holding secrets. That is not the point! You are endangering your health! You shall return to Tal Lashar now."

"No. Samantha needs time. She can't go with me now and I won't leave my beloved again. We both know what happened the last time I left my beloved alone on the lands."

Sadb never came back to me. I won't let history repeat itself.

Melise releases a sharp exhale. "Samantha isn't Sadb. She isn't pregnant or a member of a savage coven."

Except as a human, Samantha is even more fragile than a witch.

"For Poseidon's sake, return to Tal Lashar. You can meet your beloved afterwards if time is what she needs."

"No. Samantha is injured and alone in these lands. I won't leave her. I have everything under control, Melise."

"You grumpy, impulsive jellyfish-brained man, I swear–"

"Is my domain doing fine?" I ask.

"It is indeed. The improvement in your mood reflected into the North Atlantic Sea and the number of sharkman bar brawls and dolphin-folk mating incidents ebbed like a low tide. But for the sake of all things pearly, come back home. You can't lose your beloved, and none of us can lose you."

"I will do what I can, Melly," I say before closing the shell-phone.

She is right, yet nothing will bring me to leave my little human behind.

I walk back to the bedroom and lay on the bed beside her. My sleeping beloved snuggles into my chest, her body moulding against mine and a smile surges on her lips.

I won't lose you and you won't lose anything, Samantha. Even if I have to bend oceans and lands alike, no harm will come to you.

Forcing myself to stand up, I take my concoction and boil some water for her tea. Human hotels are impressive, equipped with everything, from water-boiling jars to boxes to keep food cold. They are only bereft of sex toys, a shortcoming my people would never tolerate, especially not my sister.

Once the tea is ready, I place it on the table beside her. "Baby girl, wake up to take your tea."

Opening her eyes, she sits up slowly.

"Thank you." She gives me a smile.

After probing the mug's temperature with her hands, she takes a sip, frowning at it.

"When we are in the Queendom of Tal Lashar, it will be better. There, males are the ones to take contraceptives."

"And I thought I couldn't like that place more." She releases a melodic, sleepy giggle.

I am delighted that, despite her drowning experience, she is fond of my home.

"This is due to the seahorse culture, but it is something sound, since males are always fertile while females have a short fecund window."

93

"God bless the seahorses!" She giggles, emptying the mug's content.

Now that she is fully awake, we spend hours in each other's arms, talking about Tal Lashar, her life, songs and plans. The conversation with her flows as easily as the music of the wind.

"Tomorrow I will go to the ballet performance of some of my little students in the park. Do you want to join me?" she asks.

"I would be thrilled to watch it with you."

I was fascinated seeing her teaching guitar, and tomorrow shall be the same. Watching this human twinning the magic she doesn't know she possesses is certainly becoming my favourite activity.

I am in love with Samantha, not only due to the intense bond uniting our souls, but for the fascinating woman she is. Once she is ready, I will flood her with the immensity of my devotion.

We spent the afternoon in the park, watching the little humans dancing in skirts resembling jellyfishes. Yet nothing was more alluring than Samantha's joy as she cheered for them. Now we head to her favourite food place.

We take our seats at a table in the corner. As I glance at the almost empty place where families share meals together, a tendril of longing swells in my chest. That's what I wanted and thought I had forever lost. Yet my hope is now renewed thanks to the miracle of life and music in front of me. My miracle. My Samantha.

With a soft humming, she absently gives me the menu. Is she singing my soul-song under her breath? This is the loveliest thing I've witnessed.

"You should try the salted-caramel milkshake. No, wait... you are a chocolate guy."

"If it's covering your naked skin, it is my favourite treat." I look at her over the menu and she blushes but smiles.

"No nip-licking in public," she says, hiding her face behind the menu.

I laugh. "I can wait, little one."

I have never been a patient merman, yet for her I would wait eternities. She is worthy of it.

My eyes blink and I sink my face between my hands as a piercing headache hits me. When I open my eyes, my vision tunnels, dark dots surging in front of me. I squint my eyes and some light comes in. The witch-elixir is not working!

"So, two milkshakes for here and one to go? You have to try the burgers too. I don't come here very often because it's not that cheap, but this is the best place and they have the best double cheeseburger I've t–Collins, are you okay?"

Samantha lets the menu fall on the table and races towards me. With her hands around my chin, she lifts my face to survey it.

"You are turning blue! Is it normal? God, you are so cold. Are you feeling alright?" She rushes out the questions, worry clear in her glassy eyes.

"Those are the side effects of the potion I took to have legs." I keep the wince out of my voice to not frighten her further.

"Side effects? Oh my God! Should I take you to a hospital? A bathtub? What should I–"

I take her hand in mine, halting her frantic movements to check on my pulse and temperature.

"If I don't return to the Under the Sea Queendom, my pearl will teleport me there. Samantha can you–"

"I am not leaving you, Collins! I need to make sure you are okay and nothing bad happens, even if it means facing gigantic waves." She quivers as she says the last words.

I have to find a way back to the sea before my pearl brings me there, and I am forced to leave her behind. Another wave of pain radiates from the back of my head to my spine, and my eyes clench shut at its intensity.

"Your pearl... Can it teleport me there too? Or teleport us somewhere closer to the beach?" Her voice filters through the agony and I hold her small hand, focusing on her song like a beacon amidst the darkness threatening to cover my sight.

"No. Merfolk can't teleport except in harrowing situations. Then we can only return home without taking anyone, not even our beloveds, along."

"So we need to reach the nearest beach? Would that do?"

After I nod, she helps me to stand up and we dash to the door of the eatery. As we reach the streets, cold sweat trickles down the sides of my face, and I rein in the pain, concentrating on stepping ahead.

"I will call a cab." With an arm around my waist to steady me, she raises her hand to halt a yellow vehicle.

My trembling hands reach for my shell-phone, and opening it with difficulty, I dial Melise's name.

"Collins, I was about to shell-call you, for I had this feeling–"

I cut her off, my tone clipped. "Melise, low the tides, part the seas to open a path of land. Do whatever is under your power but create a wave-free pathway for my beloved to walk to the queendom's portal."

"Collins–"

"The collateral effects are worsening. We are driving there now in one of those wheeled boxes."

"I will figure something out and get Doctor Lobstovsky ready for you. If you are coming, your predicament must be indeed serious." She sighs.

"It is."

Samantha steers me towards the mobile box, and we sit as it bolts. I cannot comprehend the words she says to the driver, but once she sets my head on her shoulder, the pain retreats a tad.

"We will be on the beach in a few hours. Try to rest."

"I regret that you have to go through such a harrowing predicament, little one."

96

"Don't. I can take care of you as well, like you do for me. Now, for God's sake, you should have told me about it earlier… Anyways, forward we go, big one." She places a kiss on my forehead and whispers, "Moronic fish!"

Even through the pain, I cannot help but laugh at her words.

My eyes close, and in a matter of minutes, I fall into a restless slumber.

The magical waters from the Queendom of Tal Lashar surround me, and my gaze rivets on Sadb's freckled face. She is in my arms, a hand placed on her swollen stomach. I run my fingers across her lovely bump and our daughter kicks in response, drawing a smile to my lips.

"I will fetch her and be back in a couple of days. I can't stay away from her any longer," she says with a sigh.

She has told me plenty about her daughter. Despite being anxious about her own fragile health condition, she is excited to meet the child from her first marriage. I too look forward to meeting her little ray of sunshine.

Sadb had intended to fetch her daughter to live under the sea with us a couple of weeks after we met. Yet her unexpected pregnancy frustrated her plans. Now she is apart from her oldest child for far longer than any mother would want. Although we both know certain risks are inherent to a trip to the land, I can't ask her to stay away from her firstborn for the couple of months she needs to give birth and recover from it. The pregnancy has been strenuous, and she only had a respite in the last few days.

"I know. Come back in haste, my love. Lingering away from the sea is dangerous." My gaze darts from her stomach to her weary face. Even with dark circles under her eyes, my air-elemental witch is a vision.

"I won't stay away from you a second beyond the necessary." Sheer conviction vibrates in her words.

All of a sudden, piercing coldness shoots into my bloodstream. The waters surrounding Sadb grow dark until she is swollen by distance. Her face disappears as though evaporated in a shallow puddle, her song quieting with every heartbeat.

The dream is broken as a haunting silence assails my senses. My eyes part, but my vision is blurry and I only can hear a whisper of Samantha's sweet soul-song.

A thick mist spreads around my mind, fogging my thoughts.

Despite her promise, Sadb never came back, and I am about to meet the same fate. My soul-song will be forever muted. A delirious thought assaults me; perhaps in death, once my soul dissolves into seafoam, a note of my song will remain and I can meet Sadb again.

Except, I don't want to meet Sadb in a preternatural plan. I want to stay alive to be with Samantha. My little human is all the music I long for.

CHAPTER 12
Samantha

I hold Collins' hand, which is warmer now. To my relief, his arms are also not going smurf-blue anymore.

He was far better for the rest of the way. Thank God we are almost arriving at the beach. To be faster, we are going the whole way by taxi and though it costs an arm and a leg, Collins has the cash on him.

I can't believe he didn't tell me about these collateral effects before. Was he trying to protect me by keeping me from worrying about him? No one has ever done that for me. It is as sweet as it is idiotic.

Noticing that his hand is once again growing cold around mine, I study his blanching face. "Collins?"

He whimpers, "It was not supposed to escalate this fast... the pain."

"I think those things are unpredictable." My arms wrap around his broad shoulders and I gently bring the bulky man towards me, giving him my warmth.

To soothe my nerves, I repeat to myself. *We are almost there. We can do it on time.* He won't die, right? He can't!

Plus, I am a little relieved that if it gets much worse, his pearl will take him under the sea, where he will feel better. My heart tugs at the idea of being away from him. The feeling is all-consuming, far greater than it is supposed to be with someone I met a week ago. Even though there is no sound explanation to the way my heart swells and why I am a chaos of passion and music when I am around him, I have to accept that this isn't an infatuation. This isn't anything less than … love. I've fallen.

"We will be *home* soon," I whisper to him.

He only reacts with a soft whimper. His fists tighten and shoulders stiffen. Is he holding back his moans of pain for my sake?

God! This merman is surreal, and I can't help but appreciate his efforts. I press a kiss on his cold temple, cuddling his large body as much as the seat belt allows.

For the final minutes of the ride, Collins grows even colder, whimpering and mumbling incoherent words. So, as soon as the cab stops, I pay and rush to help Collins out. With an arm around his back, I help steady him. I have to bite my lip to stifle the wince as I put my weight on my ankle to walk.

In a few long minutes we arrive at the deserted beach, the shore bathed by moonlight and the calm waters a contrast to my racing heart.

Drawing a deep breath, I steer him to the ocean. "We are almost there," I reassure Collins.

"The tide… did Melise?" he asks.

Confused, I look between him and the water, only to realise that the sea level is far shallower than it is supposed to be. But it's what I see farther ahead that steals the words from my lips.

"Oh my God! The sea is parted!" I gasp, following the passageway between two enormous walls of water.

"For you, so you aren't afraid…" His voice isn't louder than a whisper, as quiet as the song exuding from him.

Tears well in my eyes as my heart thrums quicker, overwhelmed by an unknown level of tenderness. He asked Melise to do it for me when they were on the phone? I was so high on adrenaline that I didn't hear a peep from their conversation.

"Thank you."

Collins replies with a whimper, and I try to hurry our steps.

"We are almost there."

"Here, come!" A melodic voice echoes from the water as a hole forms on one of the sea-wall sides. From there, Melise's upper body leans forward, and she beckons us to come closer.

"Take this, Samantha, and you will be able to breathe and speak underwater." A distraught Melise hands me the same little shell she did last time and I drink its content. "We will be at the palace soon. We just have to cross the Gulf gate and then the Atlantic portal," Melise tells Collins, her voice laced with irritation and desperation.

With her arms around Collins, the mermaid pulls him into the water, and I follow them. After passing a narrow gate, we come across the lilac and blue portal I've crossed before. Is its light duller now?

A tendril of fear has my heart in a chokehold as the memories of drowning pop in my mind. My lungs try to pull in some air, but it is to no avail and I cough some water out instead. I can't breathe.

"Samantha." Collins turns around with difficulty, stretching his arm to take my hand in his.

The touch is enough to send a ripple of warmth down my spine and soothe my unease. Trying again, I'm able to take a few shallow inhales and my breath slowly starts to even out.

"You need to go back—?" he starts, struggling to keep his eyes open.

"No! I can do it." I won't leave him.

"Come on, dear," Melise encourages me.

I nod, crossing the portal with them to arrive at the large hall of gates.

"Breathe," Collins coaxes.

One, I take a deep inhale. Two, breath in and out. Three, exhale.

We swim along the ample hall before reaching a flight of stairs. With a loud whimper of pain, Collins lets go of my hand.

"Poseidon riding a wheel of eels! That's far worse than what I have imagined." Melise speeds up, fluttering her now icy-blue tail like a rocket. Even swimming as fast as I can, I am unable to catch up.

Melise halts when they reach a man with a lobster bottom. A lobsterman?

I stop counting in my head, my fright replaced by worry and a pang of confusion. As I swim closer, I watch their chaotic interaction.

"Doctor Lobstovsky, haste!" Melise motions to the door in front of them.

"Holy Crab!" the doctor exclaims after taking a single look at Collins.

Melise opens the door and gets inside, leaving her brother with the doctor.

Why doesn't Collins feel better now that we are under the sea? Was it too late? My God! A different and far sharper kind of terror wraps around my chest, making my breath stutter. But I keep swimming. I have to remain strong for myself and for him.

Doctor Lobster frantically moves the red legs attracted to his tail to usher a handful of merfolk coming from the room towards my... towards Collins.

"Someone shall call the nymph to inform me when those appendages will disappear," the doctor says, eyeing Collins' legs.

When I finally reach them, the merfolk are circling a pale Collins, examining him and asking questions. He doesn't reply or even focus his eyes on them.

His gaze darts to me, and his murmur is so soft that if I were a foot behind, I wouldn't understand it. "Sadb."

I freeze in place, my head reeling and heart thumping faster than when it was hit by panic.

102

That's his first soulmate's name.

He is calling for her.

He sees her when he looks at me.

"Are you coming, human?" a shrimp-tailed man asks.

"I-I will come later," I say in a clipped tone, half-absently.

It was all a lie. It was just a dream. I am not the one he wants. I turn away, and swim without looking ahead, lost in my thoughts.

Did he think about her every time he looked at me? Was I his consolation prize after he lost Sadb? I huff at myself, kicking the water faster as if it was the enemy. Letting out a humourless chuckle, I hit the water with my limbs. I've always known it was too good to be true.

Plain-Jane girls like me don't get to end up with a bulky, fish-tailed prince charming. Just like with my mother's, my little-relationship-illusion came to an end, falling from a cliff. It was always bound to happen. So why am I still shocked? No, I am not shocked... but rather, confused?

I head downstairs, trying to make my way back to where I came from. I won't leave before knowing he is better, but I also can't stay close when her name is plummeting an unbearable weight into my mind.

"Sadb. It has always been her," I say under my breath.

For the sake of my sanity, I don't understand. Why, although my mind is a war zone between broken-expectations and betrayal, my heart gets warmer when I say her name?

It is as if my heart is in denial and it cannot feel cheated. I am losing it! A thud attracts my attention and I finally acknowledge my surroundings—a tall shelf, a counter and something that looks like a beer tap. Am I in a bar? The sound of breaking objects gets louder and a coral-chair flies from the adjacent room to the one I am in.

"Peace! Please, stop boy-os or I will have to call the guardian," an octopus-man says behind the counter.

He is your classic hipster with a man-bun, long beard and glasses without actual glass. To complete the look, he wears a plaid flannel scarf and has a fedora hat hanging from one of his thick tentacles.

My eyes dart between him and the couple of sharkmen barrelling towards the exit before they decide to bulldoze each other. A third sharkman rushes through the door, stopping a few steps behind me. His powerful movements send a rush of water towards me and almost cause me to lose balance. He looks feral, fuming with rage.

Jesus! Things are about to go crazy. I try to reach the door, but the sharkman is unmovable, blocking my way.

"Excuse me, can I go out?" Craning my neck forward, I ask just to be ignored.

Without acknowledging my presence, the three of them take a fighting stance, circling each other in slow-motion. Which shoots icy-cold fear into my veins and a cold ball of anxiety forms in my stomach.

I can neither fight nor flight. I am caged in by those giants. Trying to keep my nerves in check, I glance at the gaping octopus-man, who is as paralysed and helpless as I am.

Everything happens dizzily quickly. Almost shoving me against the shelf, they collide against one another headfirst, their large grey fins stirred and ready for the attack. I look at the sharp spikes on their fins and swallow. If these hit me hard enough, it can cause severe damage or worse.

"Oh my God!" I squeeze my eyes shut, this close to saying Collins' name almost in a prayer as well, hoping against all odds that he will show up. He won't.

I say through trembling lips, "Please stop."

But the rabid shark-men ignore me just like they are doing to the bartender's pleas. Their eyes are bloodshot, fangs extending down their lips and they look nothing short of possessed.

Blood charges the water after a shark-man embeds his teeth on the other one's fin. The victim jerks his tail with brutal force, trying to break from the bite. Yet his violent quivering and harsh movements end up shattering tables and chairs instead.

Thuds and the smell of blood fills the bar. Shaking, I hunch my shoulders, wrapping my arms around my chest. They move their wrestling a couple of inches closer, while the shark-man behind me releases a sound similar to a battle-cry.

So, this is how I die, as a casualty of a sharkman bar brawl? I can already picture my epitaph. *Here rests Samantha, or what is left of her. She wished she would have gone after too much chocolate and orgasms combined, but instead the first time she set foot in a bar, a shark-brawl dispatched her.*

I shake my head, a little impressed by where my horror in the face of death took me. No! I refuse to die this way. I have to act. I see a thick stick on the bar counter resembling a baseball bat and my fingers itch to collect it and use it as my defence weapon. If only I were close enough to grab the bat.

I try to scoot aside, but there is no leeway for me to move. Before I can scoot an inch away, a heavy shark-tail is about to hit me. Out of instinct, I extend my hands mid-air and the water shifts. A pulse sends both the shark-man in front of me and the one behind several feet away. The force propels my body back and out of the bar.

"Only this time, child," a warm and familiar voice murmurs within me.

The sharkman sent out of the bar with me, flashes me an apologetic look, then races away. Somehow, I ended up winning my first bar brawl. Rising, I look around and realise that the hipster octopusman is approaching me, wearing an expression of worry.

"Are you alright, human?"

I nod. Now that the adrenalin rush is dropping, I try to recover my wits.

The octopusman glares at the two sharkmen still in the bar, now broken apart and looking at me with shock in their eyes.

Standing tall like he was unable to mere minutes ago, the octopus-bartender jabs at the air with his finger and orders, "Out of the bar now, or I will call both the guardian and the queen! Brutes!" He turns to me, his gaze softer. "Are you a pet or part of someone's harem? Are you lost, human girl?" He winks, a flirty smile creeping up on his lips.

I resist the urge to roll my eyes at his pickup line and gasp at the pet part. That's offensive, but probably fair enough since humans have pet fishes.

"I can find my way. Thank you."

I walk down yet another large hall, trying to regain my bearings and make sense of my emotions and of what happened. The voice. The feeling. The power flowing in my veins for what felt like a millisecond.

My brain is protesting and trying to find some logic to it when there is none, but I am not jealous of Sadb, not when I am almost sure the voice I heard belonged to her. She protected me.

A wide-eyed Melise dashes towards me. "Here you are. I am sorry. I was so focused on Collins that I left you alone." She laces her arm with mine and I sigh, comforted by her presence. "Who would say you would end up in a bar?"

My curiosity piques between my confusion and nerves. "Do you have many bars in the palace?"

"We have, indeed. There is a bar in each wing of the palace. This is the North Atlantic wing, and an extension of Collins' domain. If you want some heady-bubbles, I can ask a shrimp to bring you a pint. So, you are a stress-drinker like me?" A smile curves her lips. "How wonderful! We will have lots of bubbles together, for men are stress-sticks with dicks and I do have plenty of them in my harem. You only have Collins, but I am sure it's a match for my forty gentlemen lovers."

I can't help but laugh. Even when Melise is worried, there is a joyful energy coming from her that automatically puts me at easy.

"How is he?" I ask, not knowing how long I spent roaming around lost. It could even have been an hour.

At this moment, I don't care about Sadb or that Collins doesn't want *me*. All that matters is him, his health, his life.

Gods of the sea, please help him!

Melise looks away for an instant and panic rises in my chest, sending a dash of adrenaline through my veins.

"Nothing is certain yet. We have to wait and see how his situation progresses. The next few hours are crucial. Now, he is awake and asking for you."

"For me?" I furrow my brows.

"Of course, my dear. He took many risks and bent the sea for you. Who else?"

Realisation dawns in my chest, crushing me with the full force of a high tide. I gasp as my doubts melt away. He bent the oceans for *me*. He took great risks for *me*. And now he is sick. He might lose his life, I might lose him.

Except I can't. I *cannot* lose him.

A sense of déjà vu has my stomach twisting and a large wave of panic plummeting on my chest. I clench my eyes, covering my face with my hands.

"Samantha, dear? Are you okay?" Melise's voice is distant, the sound muffled by the loudness in my mind, as if a thicker layer of water separated us.

"I need to see him."

CHAPTER 13
Collins

I wake up searching for Samantha, yet she is nowhere to be seen. My sister went to fetch her and they should be back soon. But unease blossoms in my chest, for I remember how I called her amidst my fever. I called her Sadb. I still can see the shock and disbelief widening her eyes.

I will forever treasure the memory of Sadb, yet I do love Samantha. I've quickly fallen in love with the brave, generous and sweet little human I've got to know beyond the soulmate-bond and any insistent reminiscence of my former beloved. *Samantha is my present and future.*

After adjusting the cables connecting me to a heart monitor among other machines, Doctor Lobstovsky clears his throat to attract my attention. "Guardian Collins, according to the nymph, your tail shall reappear in a matter of minutes, replacing those… appendages. Fortunately, we treated you in time before your condition worsened further and those legs remained."

"Sweet baby crab! Only imagining those legs would replace your tail," a mermaid nurse adds, staring at my legs in horror.

The doctor grimaces at her before focusing back on me. "We have to see how you react to the treatment in the next couple of days. For now, you must rest and take the elixir." The doctor hands me the vial containing the medicine.

Besides returning home, Melise's healing magic—a treat only she possesses in our family—and the doctor's elixir against water-deprivation were enough. They subdued my headache and the numbness stretching across my bottom-half and pearl. At least for now, as the doctor stated. If I had used the potion for longer, the effects would have been catastrophic, like my sister already emphasised.

"The beloved-bond magic also might help to improve your reaction to the treatment and avoid any long-term side effects. Neither science nor magic can fully grasp the effects of the bond, for it transcends them both."

"Thank you, Doctor."

The connection between beloveds is indeed extraordinary. I need Samantha, her presence, her song, the look in her eyes. Above that, I *need* her happiness and well-being. Thus, regardless of how much I want to, I cannot ask her to stay.

As if on cue, she and Melise enter the room. My whole being is captivated by Samantha's presence. I watch her with full attention, noticing that instead of anger or hurt, only relief gleams in her eyes. She rushes to the side of my bed, arms draping around my shoulders.

"I was terrified." She buries her face in my shoulder, and the song exuding from her swells in a nervous rhythm.

There is something rather different in its base notes. They almost seem like... I close my eyes, tightening my hold around my little human.

"He is already looking a tad better," Melise chimes in, a small smile relaxing the creases on her face.

I've never seen my sister as tense as when I woke up. Her typical carefree expression was contorted with panic.

"Indeed, Your Majesty. The progress is remarkably quick. However, the symptoms were only temporarily subdued and the patient shall remain under observation for the next three days. Only then will I be able to determine if the treatment worked and what our possible courses of action are," Doctor Lobstovsky explains, his gaze shifting between my sister and Samantha.

I take Samantha's hand in mine, ghosting my lips along it. "Our travel here was impromptu, and you didn't have the chance to settle the matters you wanted. Nor did you get the opportunity to be fully convinced about coming here."

"Don't worry about me now. I am staying for these three days or until you get better. I just have to call the guys to cancel the guitar lessons." Determination vibrates in her eyes as she holds my hand firmly.

"That can be arranged. Thank you, Samantha." I dip my chin in agreement.

Exhausted and still riding the aftermath of the dizziness and pain, I wrap my arms around my beloved, pulling her tight against my chest. She runs her fingers along my body, lingering on the scales that already scatter along my legs, a sign that my tail will reappear soon.

My eyes close and I lose the sense of time as I fall into a heavy sleep.

Releasing a soft groan, I palm the bed as my body looks for hers. She is not by my side, yet her song envelops me, its notes so close that they vibrate along my skin.

Through squinted eyes, I see her silhouette next to the sea-window, a few steps from my sister's form.

"Is he going to... get better?" Samantha asks, pain shadowing her sweet voice.

"I hope so, my dear. At this moment, I cannot say for sure, like the ebb and flow of the tide, his condition improves only to get worse."

Samantha sniffs. "He can't die. This isn't fair! I fought myself, this bond and the belief that it could be true so hard. I never got to tell him how I feel and he sacrificed everything to be with me. All for nothing."

Scooting closer to Samantha, Melise drapes an arm around her shoulder.

"Don't say that. He would do everything for you without expecting anything in return. He is more stubborn than a crab and a little grumpy from time to time, but my brother would do anything for those he loves and you–"

Slumber claims me before she concludes.

I wake up with Samantha in my arms and my cock thick with need inside my tail. Pressing a kiss on the top of her head, I watch her, entranced by the mellifluous notes swelling in her song.

After two days of brief and blurry awake moments, and dreams of Samantha dangling from her silk like a sea-angel, I finally feel like myself.

"Collins," she says under her breath.

Her fingers skim along my tail, and I have to hold a lustful hiss. My little human has no idea of how greatly she affects me.

Her intent green eyes survey my face, and the lines of tension on her forehead soften. "You look better. Are you feeling better?"

With her in my arms, I am basking in delight. Before I have the chance to answer, Doctor Lobstovsky enters the room with an entourage of nurses.

His gaze shifts from my face to the heart monitor. "The patient is finally awake and the vitals are good."

Samantha stands up to give the doctor some space, and he proceeds to examine me. She stays by my side during the entire process and once the doctor says my condition has improved and I am out of danger, utter relief shines on her smile.

"The beloved-bond certainly helped your recovery. For a while, I was convinced you wouldn't make it, Guardian Collins. Without further ado, I shall leave you two alone." The doctor winks and swims out of the room with the nurses in tow.

Samantha reclaims her place beside me, hands on my now cable-free chest. "How are you feeling?"

"I am feeling well, Samantha. How is your ankle?"

"Are you seriously asking about my ankle after I saw you turn fifty shades of blue and thought I would... God, Collins! What you did is insane. That potion could have really harmed you, or worse." A frown mars her face, but I don't miss the tears welling in her eyes.

"I am very sorry for frightening you. After one loses who they love the most, they understand that there aren't risks high enough, or limits in what they would do to stay with their families."

I would go through any perils and tribulations to both ensure she is safe and stay with her.

Samantha's grimace contorts into an expression of surprise, her lips parting. "Family?"

"You are more than family to me. You are my soulmate, Samantha. I will do anything to keep you protected and content. I would go through great lengths not to lose you."

"Am *I* the one you want, Collins?"

I release a sharp exhale. This is a fair question, considering what she heard. Despite my willingness to appease her and dispel her uncertainty, I cannot lie and deny what Sadb means to me.

She removes her arm from my chest, but I hold her back to me, drawing her undivided attention.

"Yes, you are the one I want. There is no shadow of doubt. I loved Sadb and I will always cherish what we had together. But I love *you*--your song, your smiles, who you are. I love you, Samantha."

She gasps, her breath stuttering. "I-I love you too."

After bringing her closer, I press my forehead against hers. Her song rises to a beautiful crescendo, thick with the same emotions thrumming in my chest—sheer joy, relief and hope.

She smiles as tears trickle down her face, only to blend with the large mass of water surrounding us, delicate bubbles coming from her nose. In our Queendom, the waters follow a law of their own, enveloped by magic.

My fingers twine with her white-blonde locks as I angle her face to take her lips in a longing-filled kiss. An unfamiliar yearning builds in my soul, to unite our songs as one and have her forever.

CHAPTER 14
Samantha

The love vibrating in his song, words and touch dissolve the remainder of my doubts. My fears have no reason to be.

I won't live in Sadb's shadow. Somehow, I don't even think it's possible. Sadb's memory was never a threat or an issue, but part of our path.

I won't repeat my mother's story. I know Collins and I are different from my mum's boyfriends and her. Yet it is hard to understand that something is possible when I grew up seeing otherwise. It's almost impossible to accept being loved when life has shown you the sharp claws of indifference so often that you start to believe you are not good enough. But Collins' love is greater than the tides he raised for me, leaving no space for my denial.

I kiss Collins, straddling his waist just above his gorgeous tail. A little over a week ago, I learned that magic exists. Now I know that it's not only magic, but *this* also exists. And whatever is happening between us feels like something beyond magic, as if made of stars with the sole purpose of switching the axis of my entire universe. I am breathing underwater. I am breathing him.

He pulls me closer, his kisses trailing down my neck as he cups my butt.

"You–?" I am not sure what I am asking, but I know what I want. I need him, all of him.

"I am feeling well enough to devour you completely, little one." He blows the words against my neck, shooting warmth down my stomach straight to my clenching pussy. Yes, please! Devour me.

A sudden need surges in my chest, and the words leave my lips. "How does a mark work? Something within me is urging for it, but I am–" I stop in my tracks.

I want to be with him, stay here for more than three days, move here for good. Even after the bar brawl, this place feels more like home than anywhere else ever felt. I will miss Olivia, the aerial silk, and guitar classes. Truth be told, I will miss Mum and Kimberly as well. But there isn't a choice to be made. This is my place, my life, where I can be fully present, because here is where I belong. My home is this man, his arms and his realm of incredible creatures where the impossible is always bubbling.

Collins tilts my chin to level our gazes. "Are you unsure about forever?"

Another stream of words flow without passing by the filter of my brain, "I am sure. I am just still afraid to lose you again."

Again? What am I even saying?

Collins' forehead creases in confusion, but he doesn't question it. Good, because if he did, I wouldn't know what to say.

"You won't lose me, ever. And I won't lose you. I will keep you protected and safe by my side, Samantha." His words carry the gravity of a vow, washing my heart over with reassurance.

"I want you," I breathe out the words.

A smile stretches on Collins' face, but instead of kissing or touching me, he cradles me against his chest and leans up from the bed.

"According to what I've come to learn, after I mark you, half of my pearl will reside on your collarbone and our souls will unite in the same symphony. You will live a very long life, for I will share my lifespan with you," he says as he speed-swims out of the room.

Like a koala-bear, I hold onto him. If I fall while moving at this speed, it won't be pretty. But who am I kidding? He won't ever let me fall.

"Does it mean that the years you have left to leave would be split in half?" I ask.

"Yes."

My eyes grow wide in shock. "But you–"

"Don't you understand that an existence without you is not a life? Eternity is only a burden without a soulmate to share it with."

"I do." I know loneliness and longing very well and an eternity of them seems unbearable.

With rapid flutters of his powerful tail, we cross a coral-filled hall.

"Where are we going?" I ask, peeking over his shoulder as we enter an unknown part of the palace.

"To a place I can court your properly. Afterwards, I will claim you the way I've wanted to since I saw you for the first time, regardless of how I denied it myself." His warm breath caresses my ear and his sexy tone ruins my panties.

My confusion grows as we arrive at a large oval hall. There is nothing there besides a large coral sofa and a table. It takes me a second look around to spot the beautiful pearly harp on the back of the room.

Stopping by the harp, Collins places me on my feet and collects a few blue ribbons from the musical instrument.

With a slight curtsy, he bows in front of me. "My sweet and brave Samantha, do you accept my courtship?"

"I do." My heart thrums with anticipation, warmth spreading across my chest.

Following his motion, I outstretch my arms for him to wrap the ribbons around. After a closer look, I realise those aren't ribbons but firm seaweed embedded with delicate pearls. The bracelets gleam for a moment as they touch my skin.

So that's the courtship ritual of Merfolk?

He heads to play the harp. As soon as his fingers strum the strings, purple and blue lights pop around the room and my body tingles as if sensing the magical energy caressing it.

The soft melody, resembling a classic piece, loops into a crescendo as jellyfishes come from the large square gaps around the hall. Their delicate bodies swirl with the song.

With his blue-purple eyes intent on me, he transitions to another song. My heart thuds in the rhythm of the ethereal notes I could recognize anywhere. He is playing his soul-song to me.

Yet this time, the song is a little different. There is a new upbeat touch to it.

It's beautiful, perfect and full of hope.

Tenderness and desire replaced the usual said keys.

My body moves of its own accord, and as if possessed by the cadence of his soul, I dance for him. Collins swims closer to me, his arms latching around my waist to bring my body towards his. To my surprise, the music doesn't stop. The harp is now playing on its own, attuned with the beat of his heart.

With our gazes locked, we dance to the melody of his soul. As the song swells, he lets go of my waist to take my hand in his, swirling me before swimming around me in circles.

Around us, a school of colourful fish flutters in a concentric circle. The soft end of his tail runs across my skin, stirring goosebumps. I can't stop smiling, consumed by the music and his enticing dance.

When the song stops, Collins captures me into his arms, dipping me to brush his lips on mine.

It shouldn't have stopped that soon. A few notes of the song are missing. Is it because of the leg-giving potion he took? Did it mutilate his song?

"Your song is incomplete." Worry laces my voice.

"Merfolk gift their intended with coral bracelets and a feast, dancing around them. Yet the final part of the courtship, in which I bare the totality of my song, is between us. Only you shall partake every note of my soul-songs, even the milliseconds of silence between them. Knowing someone's silence is having the map to their soul, and it is sacred. It's for you alone, Samantha. Afterwards, our songs will unite in a symphony that nothing in life can break apart."

Music flutters in my chest, as if his fingers were strumming the strings of my heart. I want that and his mark. I crave and *need* an eternity with Collins.

A swarm of fish swim into the hall, followed by a few merfolk and from the corner of my eyes I see Melise and others placing food on the table. That's the feast Collins mentioned.

An octopusman and a few crabs swim to the instruments to play cheerful music.

Melise flashes us a bright smile, gesturing to the large table, filled with dishes I don't recognize, besides the flavoured-bubbles and small crustaceans I've been eating in the last few days. They were surprisingly delicious.

Melise approaches us, brushing her fingertips on my new bracelets. Her touch makes them gleam as though their magic come to life.

"I am delighted for you both!" She presses her hands together in front of her chest, her tail gleaming in an intense shade of gold. "Should I ask the crab band to play the mating songs as well?" she asks her brother before shifting her gaze to me. "Samantha, dear, it's said that when they play for a couple, harmonising it with the few notes of their soul-songs the crabs can hear, real *stirring magic* happens. The male sticks rocket under their tails, re—"

"No. That won't be necessary, Melise. Thank you," Collins dismisses her.

"If you trust your abilities, suit yourself." Melise shrugs, taking what looks like sea-weed cookie in her hands to nibble it.

After Melise finishes eating, I hug her, and her arms wrap around me. "Thank you for the feast, for your words when I needed them the most... for everything."

"You are the most welcome, my dear. We merfolk do everything for our families." Leaning forward, she whispers in my ear, "I've left a little surprise in your room. I would normally have it here, but my brother is being a grumpy prude lately."

I nod, concealing how my nerves flutter at her words. *Prude. Surprise.* Something naughty is waiting in the room.

After eating and dancing surrounded by merpeople and fish, Collins ushers me down a long hall. Heading upstairs, we return to the same area of the palace we've been sleeping in, but he takes me to another room. The enormous bedroom has a large window from where I can see a crowded city. Without letting go of his hand, I admire the view. Shell-shaped houses and larger buildings stand between coral gardens. Merfolk with colourful tails of all shapes swim around, between schools of fishes and other eye-catching creatures.

"This place is stunning," I say under my breath.

Once Collins spins me around, I can't escape the grasp of the desire and love glimmering in his gaze. I don't have eyes for anyone else but him. My blood blazes with need. I can't wait any longer. I wrap my legs around his waist and I kiss him as my fingers hook at the hem of my top to remove it.

Scooping me up in his arms, he swims away from the window and places me on a large shell-shaped bed.

Hovering over me, he removes my fitting tank top. His intense gaze is fixed on my exposed skin.

"I won't share you with anyone. This is for my eyes only." Oh, crap! I haven't thought about it. People would be able to see us from

119

the other side of the window. "For our eyes only," Collins adds, motioning to the pair of mirrors—one on each side of the bed.

With a quick movement, he turns me around as his hand slides under my yoga pants and underwear, cupping my pussy. The hardness inside his tail pokes at my butt. How could I ever doubt his cockiness… ahem, that he has a dick?

"Eyes on the mirror as I make you come, beloved. When you are ready for me, I will share more than my soul-song with you."

"What is it?" he asks. I follow his stare to the side table, where a coral-basket stuffed with funny looking odd objects sits. "Melise! Of course, she had to do that." He shakes his head, chuckling.

Bringing the basket close, he shows me two small starfish-shaped toys. His fingers drift down my breasts, circling my nipples before giving them a teasing tug.

"Those go here." He strokes the toy against my pebbled nub before placing it there.

The object clamps onto my sensitive skin, and the ounce of pain quickly turns into pleasure. I moan, letting my head fall back. With his erection pressed against my butt, and a firm hand around my waist, he does the same with my other nipple. *It hurts so good.*

I gasp when the toy starts vibrating, sending a delicious buzz straight to my clit. Before I can recover from the little startle, Collins parts my legs to pull my pants and panties down, leaving me bare and open for him.

With a firm hand on my stomach, he pins me down, setting his face closer to my gushing sex. How can I still be lubricated under water? Is that because of magic, some kind of spell? Collins' tongue parts my folds, dissolving all my thoughts and converting them into an irrational sea of desire.

I moan, bucking against his face. This time I am not shy, but completely open to his touch and the pleasure he can give me. I am his. He is mine.

"Collins, I—"

"Eyes on the mirror, little one." He slaps my pussy, and my body arches in a wanton reflex.

In this position, I can't take a good look at the mirrors, so I prop myself on my elbows.

"There is also a mirror above," he murmurs against my pussy before licking me from clit to butt.

"Oh my… Collins!" I cry out, eyes fixed on the ceiling mirror, reflecting my sprawled image.

"Open wide and watch me eating this pretty pussy like the good girl you are."

My sex clenches at his words and I do what he says, looking at how he laps at my folds before thrusting his tongue into me. His thumb circles my clit, fingers parting my pussy. He replaces his tongue with his finger, licks down my inner thigh, then looks up. Our gazes meet in the mirror, stirring him to take me faster.

"See how wet you are for me, how beautiful you are taking my fingers."

"Yes." I can't take my eyes off his skilled fingers, diving into my pussy. In my imagination, I replace his digits with something thicker, bigger and a jolt of desire flows to my coiled womb.

Collins sinks his face into my core, licking and nibbling at my clit and folds until his tongue settles on my sensitive spot. His caresses gain tempo as his fingers work fast. This, together with the buzzing toy, sends me over the edge. My moans rise into yelps while I squirm, fingers grabbing his dark hair.

"Stunning." He props himself on his forearms, licking his moistened lips.

After pressing a kiss on my mound, he crawls up. My nipple stings when he pulls the toy off. He licks my peak, sucking it into his mouth to nibble and lap at my tender skin.

His tongue trails up to my neck, and he plugs the vibrating clamp back in place, making me tremble.

121

Collins cradles my face, gaze intent on mine. His pearl shines, and eyes are darker with lust, but his smile is something else—full of adoration and happiness. He is so beautiful.

"I need you inside me," I say under my breath.

He brushes his lips against mine and his tongue sweeps into my mouth. The tender kiss soon becomes heated as he sucks at my lips and explores every inch of my mouth, claiming me.

I wrap my legs around him, needing to feel his hardness closer to my drenched core, but he frees himself and swims up, hovering over me without touching. Before I can protest, his dick leaves his tail through a seam and he takes it in his fist. I gape, my gaze shifting from his face to his magical shaft.

Like he said, it's bigger now that the leg-spell is over, but not only that. The size is the less scary and alluring detail about his cock.

CHAPTER 15
Samantha

My gaze runs from his incredibly girthy head to the ripples and beads along his length. It's beautiful, like a step further in evolution. If human dicks would evolve or were made only for female pleasure, they would be just like this.

I roam my finger along his tip, coating his length with pre-cum. My tongue trails across my lip as an electric pulse of desire shoots down my spine.

"Please, I need you." And this magical cock.

"Anything you need, little one." With an almost feral smile, he pounces on me.

I don't register how it happens, but he has just captured my wrists and pinned them above my head. He teasingly runs his tip along my slit, and I buck my hips down to take him in.

Instead of entering me, he gathers me into his arms, placing me on the edge of the bed and closer to one of the side mirrors. He bends my legs towards my chest and rubs his tip up my throbbing folds again.

"Hold your legs up and look at us," he says.

Our gazes meet in the mirror before my eyes fix on his dick. While his thumb circles my clit with teasing flicks, he parts my folds with his thick head. I moan at the stretch, a delicious sensation between pleasure and pain flooding my veins.

"More." I look at his lustful eyes, and as if only waiting for my request, he thrusts all the way in.

His beads and ripples stroke my walls, reaching sensitive spots and unlocking a new level of delight.

"Collins. You feel... so good," I cry, gyrating my hips and dancing for him.

Through hooded eyes, I watch him shove his hips and withdraw. The sensual vision is delirious, adding to the searing ecstasy building within me.

Why do I have the sensation that he is holding back?

"I missed it. I missed your tight heat and how perfect you feel, little one," he groans, taking me faster. "Come for me and I will give you everything, my beloved." A promise vibrates in his words.

He squeezes my breast, pressing the buzzing clamp harder onto it and intensifying the sensation.

It feels perfect. It's too much. It's not enough. Never enough. I scream as the coil in my lower stomach feels like it's bursting, and ecstasy sinks into my veins as I come harder than before.

Collins withdraws, and before I can register what is happening, he rolls me to my back. His raspy voice in my ears is like a stroke, flaring my desire higher. "On your hands and knees."

I comply, lifting my butt for him as he opens my legs widely. I watch in the ceiling mirror as he runs his finger from my aching entrance to my butt, spreading my wetness across my butthole. The gentle touch wakes my nerve-endings, sending a delightful sensation and an unfamiliar need across my body.

"I need to claim every inch of you, beloved. Do you——"

I cut him off. "Do it. Please."

124

He collects something in the coral-basket and lifts the toy so I can see it in the mirror. It looks like a small vibrator, but its tip is filled with small vines instead of a smooth head.

"We shall prepare this tight, sweet ass beforehand. I won't wreck you."

He coats the toy and his fingers with lube and roams his thumb around my butthole in delicious circles that have my cleft clenching as if it wants to suck Collins' digit in. I need him deeper. I need him inside me—everywhere.

Slowly, he inches his thumb into my back entrance, and my body aches with a heady mix of pleasure and pain. After one more careful thrust, he removes his finger, replacing it with the toy.

He slides it into me gently and presses a button, making it vibrate in time with the clamps on my nipples. My eyes follow his movements in the mirror, and desire burns through me as I watch the toy disappear. Collins clicks on something else, and the toy stretches, as the vines rotate, spreading and contracting to tease every sensitive inch of my inner walls.

My eyes shut, and I scream as the building ecstasy melts me into a mindless puddle of need. I need more. I need him.

A soft spank on my ass makes my eyes flare open and a blissful cry leaves my lips.

"Look at how beautiful you are. How well this virgin arsehole is taking the toy."

I watch it in the mirror as he reaches forward to pull at my nipples, rolling the clamps around them. The pleasure is so sharp that I jolt out of the bed. I love these toys, but nothing comes even close to his magical cock, and I am delirious for more of it. For him to take me without holding back.

"Give me your cock, please." The words are followed by an uncontainable moan.

He chuckles and the joyful sound sends a trickle of warmth to my heart and a wave of yearning to my pussy.

"Oh, my sweet girl. I am so proud that you can now ask for what you want. And when you ask like this, I will give you *everything*."

"Please," I cry, bucking against the toy as I see my wanton body swallowing it.

Collins clicks on another button, and the toy's base stretches, locking it inside me. Instead of thrusting into me with a single slide like I am yearning for, he languidly draws his tip along my drenched entrance.

"Please. Give me it all." My voice almost doesn't sound like mine, the feverish desire making it throaty and velvety.

Collins releases another delicious laugh and leans down, pressing kisses along my shoulders and neck until his lips reach the shell of my ear. "It might be too much."

"It isn't. This body was made for you to fuck. We are soulmates, for God's sake." I guess now I can say all my inhibitions disappeared, giving place to unrestricted lust and a yearning that surpasses it. I need his soul wrapped around mine, but before that I need his magical stick.

"Very well, soulmate." He grins at me in the mirror.

Even overwhelmed by this thick haze of desire, I can appreciate how much he has changed since we met. Before, his smiles were rare and half-hearted. Now he looks as impossibly happy as I am feeling.

With a shove of his hips, he drives home, filling me to the hilt. I scream, body undulating towards him as I mumble some words I cannot understand.

His grasp on my hips is firm as he withdraws it to the tip, only to bottom out again. My eyes are fixed on the mirror, on the mesmerising vision of how perfectly we fit together.

His incredible texture caresses my pussy walls, drawing an intense crescendo of pleasure. Between moans and gasps, I rotate my hips and buck onto him, meeting his rough thrusts. As my ecstasy soars, my sex clamps around him. My muscles tense and I quiver, climbing to the top.

"You feel perfect, little one. This pussy is so eager and delectable," he groans, picking up his pace.

Our gazes meet in the mirror. His purple-blue eyes are burning with passion and love, and looking at them transports me into another dimension—another time and place, equally filled with ecstasy and fierce devotion. A place that I know is only ours, made of dreams, songs and memories dissolved into water.

He thrusts harder and a guttural sound between a groan and a growl leaves him. I gasp as his beads swell inside me and a soft suction motion sends me rocketing into a relentless orgasm. Although my eyes want to close at the intensity, I keep them fixed on his.

The suction intensifies and so does his swell as he grows even bigger inside me. The stretching only adds to the overwhelming pleasure, which has my orgasm extending into another climax—stronger, boundless, soul-bending.

My chest swells as light flashes before my eyes. I am surrounded by an overwhelming presence, as if my soul burst into pieces only to come back together more whole. A soundless yelp parts my lips. My heart races and my entire body, but the spot blending with Collins', grows numb as if all that exists is this connection. My eyes close, but I still can see his calling/claiming gaze in my mind. I feel a pull in my soul as though something wants to break through its shell and thoughtfully surface.

"Samantha, my love?" he calls.

I return to him, my eyes opening and the fog slowly dissipating. Yet the pull remains in the back of my mind, waiting to be brought forward.

"Are you alright?"

"Yes. I'm more than alright. The orgasms are so powerful that I am kind of hallucinating." I giggle, giving into another powerful wave of bliss.

The clamps, the vibrator and his deep thrusts are too much. I am at the mercy of the overwhelming pleasure he bestows and all I can do is come continually. I moan, grinding on him and gyrating my hips in tempo with his song.

Collins leans to peck soft kisses along my neck and back before pulling out. Steering me to lie on my back, he parts my legs to slide in again.

He gives me a heated smile, half-feral and half-loving. "This way, it will be more comfortable when I am locked inside you."

Before I can ask what he means by locked inside me, he takes my lips in an all-consuming kiss, his tongue moving in tandem with his cock.

Collins' movements grow unsteady. After a few thrusts, his cock jerks and fills me with warm spurts. His member swells further, and I groan at the pleasurable sting.

I wince, growing uncomfortable. My spent body can't take the vibration any longer, but Collins' cock is a different story and I need him to remain buried deep inside me. As if he can read my mind, he carefully removes the vibrator and the clamps, then he kneads my aching nipples between his fingers, drawing a soft cry from my lips.

I try to adjust my body, but I can hardly move. He is indeed locked inside me.

He motions to where our bodies join. "It will take a while for the beads to shrink. I will be tied inside you until then," he explains, running his fingers along my arm. "Granted how perfect you feel, it might last longer than normal."

"Good, I am not ready to have you outside of me."

"Neither am I ready to leave." A serene smile curls up his lips.

"Once you get used to a bigger vibrator, you will take my cock here." He reaches down to cup my butt.

I reply with a soft moan. I can't wait to be wrecked.

Adjusting me in his embrace, he kisses the tip of my nose and my cheeks before his lips touch mine in a loving kiss.

He breaks the kiss, and his fingers skate along my hair, eyes holding a look of pure adoration. "My sweet beloved, my love," he beams. "Give me your eternity, for my life is yours, and so is my soul-song."

My heart swells at his words, and I say without doubt or hesitance, "I'm eternally yours, my beloved."

I love him more than I can understand, but I've given up making sense of my emotions. Until yesterday, I was scared to surrender to my feelings in all their intensity and urgency. But when I almost lost Collins without telling him how I felt, this fear abated, opening space to a greater one—spending my life without him, wasting my life without this feeling. I had to accept this undeniable love. There was no choice but to yield to the force of the tides, just like there was nothing to do but let this love be, grow, and sing within me. Like music, love is to be felt, not thought, and logic has no place in matters of the heart.

Our lips unite, and the ever-present hum rolling off him extends into the full notes of his song. The quiet whispered keys/chords resembling a sea breeze reach a lively crescendo. His melody is even sweeter, now touched by a dash of devotion.

Pouring his love into our kiss, he gives me all—every ounce of his song and the seconds of silence between the notes. It's intimate, tender, and perfect.

His song takes root in my heart, and my music flows from the depths of my soul. The melodies complete each other, composing an incredible symphony. Warmth spreads from my chest along my body, washing me over with delicious tingles as if the song is touching my skin.

Water swirls around us in gentle circles, and a surge of colours bloom, surrounding our bodies. My senses fuse, and everything comes together—his skin on mine, his kiss, the colours and our music. It's all part of the same magical orchestra.

Two dashes bend around each other, coming closer to touch. Our songs dance together before my eyes in light and magic. Once the dim blue light completely intertwines with the icy grey one, something within me breaks free as though it wants to join the dance, wrapping itself in the visible music and melodic light.

Collins kisses me harder, urgently, resuming his thrusts as our blended song swells into a crescendo.

As I moan into his mouth, I latch my legs around him to have him closer. I need more. I need everything. I yearn for his mark.

The union of our songs weaves our beloved bond, but death still can set us apart, silence the notes of our music. I can't have that. Never again.

How do I even know that? It doesn't matter. My mind and soul are now fully possessed by this urge. I need *forever*.

"Collins," I cry out.

Without waiting, he answers my deepest desire. With a slow and deep thrust, he props himself on his forearms, so his collarbone hovers over mine. A faint glow attracts my gaze to his pearl. His eyes are intent on mine, more purple and profound than I've seen.

A droplet leaks from his pearl to the dip of my collarbone, and when it touches my skin, a surge of energy ripples through my body. An immaterial pulse within me trembles, surfacing to accept and embrace his mark. My collarbone thrums like a second heart, sending waves of electricity to my toes and the end of every hair on my head.

We are one.

I feel the totality of his soul, everything that transcends his song. His magic thrums across my skin and plays with my heart, as if it were a musical instrument.

"You are so beautiful," I say, mesmerised by his soul's solid and steady pulse. Collins' emotions—especially his love—are as endless as the sea, and now I feel it fully vibrating within my heart.

He has suffered so much, gone through decades of hopeless solitude, but made it through. After meeting me, it was as if his soul was reborn.

"You are stunning, my Samantha. You are *everything*." His eyes widen, a glassy mixture of shock and reverence in them.

130

CHAPTER 16
Samantha

Once I feel the pearl seat in the depths of my soul, white light steals my vision as a serene but confident voice stretches across my mind. "At last, time unites—present and past blend as one at the mark in your soul."

The light wanes, and a vast green meadow forms before my eyes. I run towards an old wooden well, and my gaze searches for the water. The face staring back at me is at the same time mine and another—brown hair, emerald-green eyes, and a freckle-dotted cheek.

I sway my little hand in the air, and a gust of wind follows my movement, bending at my will. Sheer joy vibrates within me as I lift little pebbles with the blow, making them dance in a circle around me.

Another flutter of my fingers and leaves join the flurry. I undulate my arms and legs, dancing with the air until my feet hover over the ground. I'm flying—such an odd and familiar sensation. I've searched for that while dancing or dangling in my silks. Without understanding, I missed being one with the air.

I swirl around, my dark hair flowing in circles hoisted by another gust. The cooling wind spirals around me, joining the dance and leaving the lingering taste of freedom.

I am an elemental witch. I can play with the winds, eliciting them to strum the stones, the leaves, and the grass until their rattling becomes a melodic song to form my very own orchestra. With a movement of my fingers, I can turn the world around into a wonder of music and dance.

"Sadb, come. Dinner is ready," my mum calls.

Giggling, I run towards a small house. My home.

As I blink, I am transported elsewhere. Places and people stream before my eyes—the cliff, my former coven, the cold grey sea, my parents, a newborn baby bundled in a blue blanket.

The images disappear, replaced by the waves crashing on the white sand. They are ebbing and flowing in a gentle rhythm.

"My beloved. My Sadb," Collins calls, combing a dark lock off my face. In response, fierce love flares in my chest.

I didn't know I could have a beloved, but my soul immediately recognised his, and his song made its home in my chest. The whispered notes resembling the sea breeze trickled into my heart, followed by the crescendo of desire. Silence and sound twined composed his striking melody.

"My Collins. My beloved."

Light and darkness swirl in my vision, and I'm back into the depths of the sea. Except, I'm Sadb instead of Samantha, and the past still stretches across my mind.

I am in Collin's arms, revelling in his comfort. My hands wander across my swollen stomach, where our child grows. I hug Collins, bidding him farewell and the promise of a quick return dangles between us.

"I will fetch her and be back in a couple of days. I can't stay away from her any longer," I say.

My heart aches for my oldest daughter, who I couldn't see for so long. I can't fully understand the meaning of my words or that moment, but the longing overwhelms my senses, permeating every inch of my heart.

"I know. Come back in haste, my love. Lingering away from the sea is dangerous." His gaze jumps from my stomach to my eyes.

"I won't stay away from you a second beyond the necessary," I vow.

Light flickers, and darkness descends upon me.

"Mum," a little girl calls me. I recognise her voice. It's my daughter.

But I can barely reply. My life energy is escaping me, dark magic consuming my flesh and stealing the warmth from my limbs.

With difficulty, I keep my eyes open, because I know all the light will be stolen from them soon. My voice is lower than the gentle morning breeze the sea blows to announce a new day. "Take care of your sister, my sweet girl. I love you both. I will come ba—" Death claims me before the last feeble word crosses my lips.

A soft shift in the air, now cold like the prelude of a storm, and I see myself floating over my body, struck by icy desolation. My daughter is on her knees, crying before me, and I can't console her.

I need to come back for my children and my beloved. I didn't care for revenge and those who wronged me. I only cared for my family, my heart.

An invisible hand pulls me from the bare room, away from my oldest daughter and my lifeless body. I am surrounded by silver light, and my soul thrums in recognition. I'm about to be reunited with the Goddess—Nyx—the infinite night and every star within, divine mother and sire of all witches.

I've seen Nyx in my prophetic dreams and visions. As the only witch in my coven with the gift of foreseeing, I have always had a special bond with my Goddess. This unique gift and connection raised the envy of other witches, sealing an ending I can't remember much about.

Yet I know that none of my visions could save me from my demise.

Gazing at Nyx's immaterial form, I say, "Forgive me, my mother, my Goddess. I can't go to you; not yet. I have to return..."

I had to right my wrongs. I shouldn't have left Collins and come to fetch my daughter by myself.

I shouldn't have trusted the coven leader. But there is no point in dwelling on guilt when one is dead.

I have to come back.

I can't leave my children and Collins. I won't let it happen.

My soul drifts away from the silver light, floating within a void as extensive as a moonless night. Without letting the Goddess' lure seep through me, I search the way back to my body. After gliding aimlessly for a while, two bright beacons guide me back to my coven. There I can listen to his song—now rustled with melancholy.

Collins isn't there in the coven. He hasn't found our little girl and rescued my children from that cruel place, taking them to live with him. Yet his sorrow ripples along the shores, turning the waters dull grey with his grief.

For a glimpse of a second, I see my children. They are older, and my body is gone. How long has it passed? A soundless scream burst in my immaterial chest. I have to find another way back.

A pitch canopy blankets me and the Goddess' voice fills my soul. "There is no going back. Time passes differently on the other side of the veil separating the living from the dead."

"I have to return to them."

"That is not your fate, Sadb," the eternal night whispers back.

"I can't follow or accept a fate that sets me apart from them. I have to return to my family," I reply.

"Then you shall both find and make your way." The Goddess's voice comes from all sides, echoing from the stars.

Within the void surrounding my desolated soul, a soft blink attracts my gaze. Prompted by the force of my love and desperation, I follow the faint gleam, and once again, I feel the warmth of life caressing the seams of my soul.

I am a life to be.

Darkness returns, heavier with uncertainty, but as my soul settles in what is to be a body, a note of his song once again shrouds me. I let it lull me and guide my way back to life.

"I won't stay away from you a second beyond the necessary," I repeat my vow before oblivion possesses my consciousness, and all surrounding me is the delicate flair of life and the familiar touch of his song—a call I have to follow.

I blink multiple times until the memories dissolve in a fog, and my eyes meet Collins's. He strokes my cheeks, wiping the tears I can shed underwater.

Tipping my chin up, he gazes deep into my eyes as if he can access my soul. Maybe he can, and that's how his mark united us.

The crystalline moisture of unshed tears coats his eyes, making them gleam in a mesmerising shade of violet-blue—deep and laced with emotion.

Recognition.

Longing.

Homesickness.

I've also spent my latest life *homesick for him.*

"You are Sadb."

"Can you see it too? Did you see all the memories unfolding?" I ask.

"I didn't see anything. I only felt two soul-songs fitting like a puzzle. Two that have always been one. A few notes changed. Alas, they always do in the course of existence. Life plays us as if we are their instruments, and our souls ricochet—vibrating, singing and occasionally twisting in response. How haven't I noticed that the songs were one and the same?" He shakes his head, but the sparkle of bemusement doesn't flinch.

I cup his face, fingers running down his cheeks. "You didn't want to cheat me with myself."

"You are my Sadb, my Samantha, my everything. My beloved."

He showers my face with gentle kisses, thrusting deep into me. Pleasure bleeds through the bewilderment, and our newly formed connection pulses in my veins and the pearl on my collarbone. It's gleaming just like Collins'.

Plenty of emotions and questions brew in my chest, but now he and our connection are the only answer I need.

Holding me tighter as if he is afraid, I will fade in the next delicate water current, he seats himself into me completely. Tingles radiate from the spot where our bodies unite.

"I am back to you—completely, two lives as one, and all I am."

He captures my lips with his, but his reply doesn't need words.

Two lives he loves. Longing pumps in the swell of his song, his pearl pulsing inside my flesh like a second heart, and his cock throbbing within me.

Collins retreats as much as he can to slide back into me in a profound and slow thrust, savouring every second of this long-awaited reunion. Since I first met him in this life—and even before—I could feel our connection unfolding, but now it is more powerful. I feel, I know and I embrace it. There is no more forgetfulness between us.

As our bodies unlock, he pulls back, but doesn't fully withdraw. He is as unwilling to break the contact as I am. Not a second or inch beyond the necessary. Enveloped by their music, our souls make love.

"Nothing will keep you away from me now." His words come out in groans as he traces the tiny pearl between my collarbones with his fingers.

The touch sends jolts of electricity directly to my clit, and it is all I need to combust in a sea-bending orgasm.

My pussy clamps around him and I scream his name as pleasure filters through all my senses, rendering me semi-liquid. Collins follows suit, emptying his spurts into me.

Without leaving my body, he flips us around. "My perfect beloved, Samantha, Sadb." He runs his fingers along my hair, cupping my nape and looking at me with sheer adoration. "What should I call you?"

"Call me *yours.*" My name doesn't matter—I am both.

I am two threads of memories, marks of the two lifetimes, intertwined to form a complex pattern of weaved recollections and dreams. A pattern that's neither Samantha nor Sadb but the confluence between them, which burns for this reunion, this returning to the home within his arms.

Although torn into two lives, I couldn't be more complete.

"Mine," he claims, with a shallow thrust. He is now half-mast and still buried inside me.

My inner muscles clench, unwilling to let him go. As if he can read my thoughts or, rather, my pussy's intentions, he replies with a chuckle. "I am not leaving our tight heat, mine."

Yawning, I snuggle further into his arms. Despite my desire to stay awake and make love again, I can hardly keep my eyes open.

"Sleep, little one. I see how weary you are. I won't leave *my* perfect pussy," he says.

I nod against his chest, drinking in his warmth and the delight of being one with him.

Exhausted by the marking and the weight of many memories, I doze off immediately.

CHAPTER 17
Samantha

Our joined songs are like a lullaby, filling my dreams and basking me in a sea of comfort and contentment. Home.

Home means everything for someone who spent a long time lost between the void of the afterlife and an existence that I couldn't reconcile with the desires of my soul—the sea, the air dancing around my fingers, my beloved's song, and my children's faces.

Two pairs of eyes follow my dreams; green and blue. My daughters' eyes. The song blanketing me reaches a wailing note as the other side of reality crashes in like a violent wave.

I left them. I couldn't return in time.

Icy guilt stretches through my chest.

All of a sudden, warmth radiates from my pearl, and the soul-song soars, rising into my ears and enveloping me like a giant wave. The heat dissolves into a peaceful darkness as the night surrounds me, pulling me out of my body and into a plan I am familiar with. The striking darkness filled only with stars. A non-place that is everywhere and has always been within me. I've visited it many times when I lived Sadb's life. Her visions and prophetic dreams took Sadb here, before Nyx.

The serene voice of the Goddess stretches in my mind again, in what I know is the last time. I am not a witch anymore. Although my soul will always be connected to Nyx, I no longer have the magic to tap into this link.

"Not while you live. And you shall live long with the soul of a song pulsating above your chest. In the meantime, that is my last visit, my child. Embrace your miracle and the life you gave yourself. Following a song that not even death could silence, you found your way back to life, bending your fate. Yet your own destiny is the only one you can bend, Sadb. You could not do it differently for your daughters, for they have their own stories and paths to follow. Forgive your past; dwelling on what could have been is a fools' errand. Life only flows forward."

I wake up with the echo of the Goddess's words caressing my ears. Collins is still deep-seated inside me.

Now that I remember, I put the pieces together. The voice I heard after the sharkman fight was the Goddess'. The pulse of energy I inadvertently released to protect myself was nothing more than a reflection of Sadb's air-bending abilities—my powers. I bent the air within the water to shove the shark and his menacing sharp fins away.

Collins cups my face, concerned eyes studying me. "Are you alright? You cried in your dreams."

"I had a dream about the Goddess, like the ones I used to when I was Sadb. A dream-vision."

I tell him everything I saw in my dream, and after his pearl touched my skin, marking me and uniting our souls—the memories, the Goddess, the emotions unfurling within me. For so long, I used to feel many of these emotions, the longing, the sensation that I was in the wrong place, living the wrong life. Only now can I make sense of them. I was in the wrong place, and my soul craved to reunite with Collins's, for the life I wanted to return to, but I was too late.

His song never stopped whispering within me since, a reminder to my soul that my mind couldn't grasp, a call and beacon to guide my way back home.

"Sadbmantha," he tries the name on his tongue, and I give him a wee smile as the memories stretch further.

Lifting my chin, he says, "The heaviness of your guilt brushes over my shoulders. I can feel whatever you do now, beloved."

"I shouldn't have gone away from the sea. I shouldn't have died," I choke back the tears.

"Beloved, you shouldn't feel guilty for dying. You couldn't have foreseen that your coven-leader would poison you with dark magic. Besides, you followed through your words and came back to me, to us." He cups my face, his thumbs wiping the trickling tears.

"I took too long, and my children…." Nyx's words return to me washing me over with a sense of peace, and I pause. *"You could not do it differently for your daughters, for they have their own stories and paths to follow. Forgive your past."*

He presses his forehead against mine, bringing my knuckles to his lips for a gentle kiss. "You bent the fates and did the impossible to return to me, to find the path back to us, Sadb. Your determination and love were so strong. You are strong and brave, little one. Beyond the beloved-bond uniting us, you made me fall in love with you in both lives and versions of you."

"I too fell in love with you twice. Although this second time I was very stubborn." A half-hearted smile forms on my lips, even as I still feel torn between joy and regret.

"Now we are reunited and you can meet your children, and hopefully continue growing our family from where we stopped." He caresses my unclad stomach. "Don't allow guilt to eat at your soul. For years I've felt guilt for failing you, and it took Melise and our daughter to convince me otherwise. That's why I couldn't leave you alone over-the-sea regardless of how the legs-brewing potion affected my health. I couldn't leave my beloved unprotected."

"I am safe, and here to stay. I won't go anywhere. I don't want to be anywhere else but here, with you."

Sweet moronic sexy piece of tail! I smile, holding tighter to him. I wouldn't hesitate to grow a tail and become smurf-blue with illness to stay by his side.

"Collins, it's not your fault."

"I am aware of that due to Melise's insistence and our daughter's words. You will love to get to know more about our little fish."

"I don't want anything more than a present and a future with the three of you." Now, I have this precious chance and refuse to ruin this miracle with a shadow of my past. "I promise, I won't blame myself," I add.

Our songs swell with a softer note as silent understanding passes between us.

"We found each other. We can begin again… we have already begun again and now that our souls are united in this mark, nothing can set us apart," I say, wrapping my arms around his neck and pulling myself closer.

The Goddess's words vibrate within me as I look intently at Collins, embracing my miracle, my *present*. That's what matters the most. It took me a lifetime, but I am back as I promised.

EPILOGUE
Samantha

I walk down the coral garden with Collins, getting reacquainted with the main street of Tal Lashar after a lifetime away. The shell buildings and colourful lawns of coral and sea-weed are as beautiful as in my distant recollections warped to the abstract form of dreams.

I spent the last few hours reconciling my lives. I called my—Samantha's—-family to tell them I won't return. Now that Mum is happy with a guy who respects her, I don't have to worry about her. But Collins promised to convert some sea treasures into money and send her a few thousand dollars every month, so she wouldn't have to depend on Wyatt for anything. This way, Mum can freely decide whether to stay with him. Kimberly was happy about the money, and for the first time, she had no complaints. I only hope financial independence can set her free of a cycle of choosing people in her life according to what they have to offer her. Yet that's her choice, not mine.

I have also bid farewell to my friend Olivia. I didn't tell her the details about my new-old life; humans aren't very welcoming to what they can't understand, which includes magic. She was glad to

143

see me finally happy and free. Once Doctor Lobster and the nymph clear Collins out to use the legs-brewing potion for another hour, we will visit her and Noah.

Collins halts in his tracks, taking my hand in his. "How about your studies? I don't want you to leave my side and the safety of this queendom, yet I won't deprive you from anything. I refuse to hinder your path to your dreams."

I know how hard it is for him to consider having me departing to the land. The fact he is doing this for my happiness is yet another token of his love. Yet my happiness resides here, beside him.

Recovering Sadb's memories changed the way I speak, feel and my priorities. My emotions are stronger, especially my desire to be with *my family*—my girls and Collins. I still want to pursue a path of dance and music, but it has to be here. It has to be *home*.

"My dance university isn't an issue. I just want to dance and lose myself in music, in your song. It has always been my favourite sound, the one to twine and reunite all other melodies. I will be happy if I continue dancing here in Tal Lashar. Maybe teaching little merfolk to dance and play guitar as well."

"They will love you. You are a brilliant teacher, and look like an angel entangled in silks," he beams.

"I hope so, I've always loved children." Especially two brunette little girls. The thought makes my eyes glassy with tears. "I want to see my girls soon." I sigh.

Collins lets go of his shell-phone, finishing texting our daughter.

He tightens his hold on my hand, thumbs caressing my knuckles. "Although our daughter is heavily pregnant, she said she can come here in a few days."

He still didn't tell me much about her and her story, but I prefer it this way. I would rather hear it from her—my chest tugs with longing. I am looking forward to meeting my youngest daughter.

"Isn't that strenuous for her?" I ask, remembering how taxing it was when I was carrying her.

I don't want her to go through an exhausting trip to meet me. I am her mother, the one who should cross oceans for her, protect and love her. I couldn't ask anything from her.

I accepted that I couldn't do it, and she has her own story to write and destiny to fulfil, but now that I am alive and I remember her, I will give her my love.

"No, she is to deliver her baby under the sea. Coming here won't be an issue. Yet I haven't told her about you via shell-phone."

Halting in my tracks, I take Collins' hands in mine and give him a small smile of gratitude. "Thank you. I wouldn't like her to know about me this way."

"How about my older daughter?"

"She cannot come."

"Can't we visit her instead, then?" I ask.

"It's a rather complicated situation, my love."

I swallow the lump in my throat, pushing the dreadful words past my lips. "I–is she–?"

"No, she is alive. Worry not. Yet visiting her now or any time soon won't be possible, perhaps when I can use the legs-brewing potion again, and only after a few precautions are taken."

Why is it so hard to visit her? My heart pounds as icy fear pumps into my bloodstream.

"My Goddess, my—"

"She is fine. You will meet them as soon as possible, rest assured." Collin's large hands frame my face as he brings my body closer to his, basking me in his warmth. "Meeting your oldest daughter might be harder, but I will make it happen. I promise you, my love."

I reach up to press my forehead against his, and his arms come around my waist before our lips touch in a sweet kiss brimmed with love.

I want to make peace with Samantha's life, to embrace it and Sadb's memory completely.

The people in Samantha's life deserve that. I deserve that.

My daughters also deserve their mother's love—something they were deprived off for too long.

I won't ever be only Samantha or Sadb, but both of them. The one who left too early and challenged the very circle of life to return guided by a song and this immense longing to live, love and reunite.

Above anything, I need to meet my children, love Collins and together compose our beautiful song of soul.

NEWSLETTER

Access to the extended epilogue, please sign up for my newsletter below:

Click Here

To read more about this world and meet some of these characters again, see below:

The Golden Dragon's Surrogate.

EXTENDED EPILOGUE
Samantha

A radiant mermaid enters the palace hall. My daughter. Her husband has an arm wrapped around her shoulders and a hand resting on her swollen stomach as he gives her a look of pure adoration. She smiles back at him, love clear in her gaze.

Her happiness soothes my heart, mitigating part of my nostalgia.

Collins told me about him and the obstacles he and our daughter faced to be together.

As soon as her eyes meet Collins, her lips stretch in a bright smile.

"Dad! It's so good to see you. I'm so relieved you are feeling better."

She swims close, taking a better look at me, and Collins squeezes my hand in reassurance, his song reaching a calming note.

"I didn't know you had found a beloved. Wait… how can it be?" She stops in her tracks, eyes widening. "Mum?"

I gasp, struck by shock.

"How do you know?" Collin asks, his expression mirroring my disbelief.

"Your soul-song. I can hear a few notes. I remember them and how they mixed with the thrum of your heart when you were carrying me," she says, approaching with quick flutters of her blue and purple tail.

Her words make my eyes well with tears as my chest swells. She recognises my song. It has changed since Collins marked me, and now, it reunites the melodies of Samantha's and Sadb's souls.

I close the gap between us, my nerves winding tight and my heart racing in tempo with my agitated soul-song. "I'm so sorry for leaving you. I would have done anything to stay, raise and love you, my beautiful girl. Can you—"

Wrapping me in a hug, she cuts me off. Her action fixes a fracture in my heart, making my soul-song soar with sheer love.

"Mum! You have nothing to be sorry for. I know what happened to you. You were poisoned with dark magic." She sniffs. Putting enough distance between us, I gently wipe off her tears. "It's in the past, and it doesn't matter any longer. All that matters is that you are back to us, to your life."

My sweet girl is taking it far better than I imagined. She has inherited her father's big heart.

"I won't leave you or your sister again. Never."

"She will be so happy to see you," my daughter says, a lovely smile lighting her crying face. My beautiful baby. The gleam in her eyes is the same from when she was a wee child.

Her words bring me great relief. Once I have her sister in my arms, my heart will be complete.

"I will give you some space," her husband says. I am looking forward to meeting him and their family after I get to know her.

Once she nods in response, he lays a kiss on the top of her head and swims away.

"Should I leave you both?" Collins asks.

"No," we say in unison.

I need to stay with both of them. They are my long-sought home.

"I am so happy for both of you. To see you smiling again, Dad, and to see you, Mum."

Mum—I love how that sounds. It's not the first time she calls me this way, yet the word has tears of delight rolling down my cheeks. Collins immediately wipes off my tears with the back of his hand, draping his arms around me and bringing my back against his chest.

"I can't wait to get to know you," she adds.

I can't recover the lost time, but thanks to Collin's pearl, I will have a long future ahead with the two of them. Well, the three of them.

"Can I?" I ask, motioning to her beautiful, unclad baby bump.

"Of course. Meet Shawn."

I place my palm on her belly, and her baby boy kicks against it, drawing a smile to my lips.

"He is excited to meet you." She smiles.

"Hello, baby." I run my fingers over her stomach, earning yet another sweet kick.

Collins places his hand on mine, a radiant smile lighting up his face.

"Holy Nyx! How is this even possible? This is a miracle. Thanks Goddess!" She takes my hand in hers, bemusement clear in her eyes.

"This is your mother's miracle, sweetheart. She challenged the cycle of life to return to us, guided by love," Collins says.

"Guided by your song," I tell him, snuggling into his embrace.

"Aren't they the same thing?" she beams.

Collins

(7 years later)

I follow our three-year-old son as he quickly crosses the hall leading to the nursery. I tried for an hour but failed to tuck him to bed.

A few months after our union, my beloved and I left the bubbling frenzy of the palace and moved to my private house in the Atlantic Sea, where Melise, my daughter and her children visit us often.

Once my beloved reunited with her older daughter, her heart was pacified and her soul completed. So, Samatha agreed to have more children and I can now live this dream of chaos and love.

The little chaos brewer chuckles, drawing a smile to my face.

"Don't make noise, Caspian. You don't want to wake your little sister up," I murmur, finally catching him in my arms, despite how quickly he flutters his green tail.

The imp little fish replies with a giggle and a naughty smile.

"It's alright, she's awake." My beloved's sweet voice comes from the room and with Caspian tucked in my arms, I enter it.

A large smile forms on my face as I come across Samantha nursing our five-month-old. The tiny mermaid moves her purple tail softly as she runs her chubby little fingers down her mother's hair.

"Layla woke up hungry." She smiles, adoration gleaming in her eyes as she watches our baby feeding.

"Mama! Mama!" Caspian jumps from my arms, swimming closer to Samantha to wrap his arm around her and his sister.

"Hello, my sweet boy! Did you and Daddy count turtles to fall asleep?"

"Yes! Five!" He shows the number with his raised fingers.

Samantha chuckles and plants a few kisses on his face before turning to look at me. The little lad quickly swims towards his shell-blocks and coral play dough to create another havoc of joy.

"I had another dream." Samantha has had many dreams about her past as Sadb and although she forgave herself for leaving her girls and me behind, the memories plummet her into nostalgia.

"About your past?" I swim closer, leaning next to her in the rocking chair, my arms draping around her shoulders as my hand roams across our tiny one's back.

"No. About our future. Well, that and our perfect present, filled with music and love."

She lifts her face to press her forehead against mine. "About home, the one I found in you and our family."

A heavenly smile forms on her lips before they brush against mine.

Her soul song swells with delight, reaching a sweet rhythm and taking mine along. After the marking, our songs entangled, yet they part at times only to be reunited again in love, song and unrestrained pleasure.

"The beautiful home I've come back to build with you," she adds, her gaze roving between me and the children.

She says I'm her home, but she is also mine. Looking at her and our little fishes, I cannot believe my fear almost prevented me from

152

making this dream come true. Samantha might have returned to life for her girls and me. Yet doing so she brought *me* back to life. Before her, existence was more silence than music, she didn't only bring back a song, but converted my life into a vivid symphony.

With quick flaps of his tail, Caspian approaches, holding some white play dough in his hands.

"Look Mama, Daddy, a pearl!" He brushes the play dough pearl close to our faces.

"It's beautiful." Samantha beams.

"Make it sing!?" he asks.

We know very well what he wants, to partake in the song of love that created this family.

Samantha runs her fingers down his dark hair as she hums our combined soul-song. It's the only sound that manages to calm the little ball of energy down or lull him to sleep, especially when his mother sings it.

He claps his hands in delight, before pressing his head on my shoulder and yawning.

I wrap my arms around my three treasures, my heart thrumming in tempo with the melody of our souls.

Our little lad closes his eyes, fully snuggling into my chest.

"She has also fallen asleep again." Samantha strokes Layla's blonde head.

I kiss our little fishes' heads, before my lips meet Samantha's, bringing our intertwined songs to the highest note—pure love and happiness.

ACKNOWLEDGEMENTS

Thank you, Vicki, for helping me edit "A Song of Soul" and to my lovely Beta readers, Hali and Nikole. This book wouldn't be here if it weren't for you.

ABOUT THE AUTHOR

T. R. Durant is a young author very dedicated to her craft, with over ten completed books. This daring novelist is now transitioning into the world of self-publishing.

Our lawyer-turned-author, whose passion for character profiles of the stories she grew up reading and creating, drove her to study psychology. She has always believed in love and magic and used to lose herself in the verses and rhythm of poetry.

Having lived in eight different countries, she is currently based in Europe, and you will always find her on https://www.trdurant.com/

Or her Facebook group:

ALSO BY T. R. DURANT

Of Fire and Light Series

The Golden Dragon's Surrogate (Book 1 of the Into Her Secrets Duet)

The Sea Witch's Beloved (Book 2 of the Into her Secrets Duet)

COMING SOON:

Envy: the Curse of Beauty—coming in December 2023.

Into Her Darkness (Megan's book)—coming in 2024.

24 Dates After Christmas—Coming in 2024.

Printed in Great Britain
by Amazon

31540758R00089